The Dangerous Lover

The Dangerous Lover

Gothic Villains, Byronism, and the Nineteenth-Century Seduction Narrative

Deborah Lutz

The Ohio State University Press
Columbus

Library of Congress Cataloging-in-Publication Data

Lutz, Deborah.
The dangerous lover : Gothic villains, Byronism, and the nineteenth-century seduction narrative / Deborah Lutz.
p. cm.
Includes bibliographical references and index.
ISBN-13: 978-0-8142-1034-5 (alk. paper)
ISBN-10: 0-8142-1034-1 (alk. paper)
ISBN-13: 978-0-8142-9111-5 (cd-rom)
ISBN-10: 0-8142-9111-2 (cd-rom)
1. English fiction—19th century—History and criticism. 2. Seduction in literature. 3. Love stories, English—History and criticism. 4. Love stories, American—History and criticism. 5. Gothic revival (Literature) 6. Antiheroes in literature. 7. Villains in literature. 8. Romanticism. 9. Byron, George Gordon Byron, Baron, 1788–1824—Influence. I. Title.
PR868.S423L87 2006
823'.809352—dc22
2006001265

Cover design by DesignSmith
Typeset in Adobe Garamond
Printed by Thomson-Shore, Inc.

The paper used in this publication meets the minimum requirements of the American National Standard for Information Sciences—Permanence of Paper for Printed Library Materials. ANSI Z39.48–1992.
9 8 7 6 5 4 3 2 1

Contents

Acknowledgments

I dedicate this book to Eve Kosofsky Sedgwick, who always gave me plenitude. I want to express my gratitude to Avital Ronell for her attempts to keep me to a line of rigorous questioning, to responsible thinking and, at the same time, to excessive ideas. And I thank her for her Heidegger: "Denken ist Danken." Anne Humpherys I thank for her limitless knowledge about the nineteenth century and for her coining of the term "dangerous lover." My warm thanks to Wayne Koestenbaum for his scrupulous attention to my writing and all its follies, and I thank him for being Wayne: irresistible. My sister, Pamela, inspires me to write by her example and by her constant encouragement. My mother I thank for her willingness to be proud of me at every turn. Benjamin Friedman, for his tireless proofreading and friendship. Yvonne Woods, Kris Badertscher, Charlotte Deaver, Melissa Dunn, Rebecca Reilly, Maggie Nelson, and Jean Mills shared with me ideas, critique, and encouragement. I thank Stella, for always bringing light.

A fellowship from the Jewish Foundation for the Education of Women gave me the time to finish the bulk of this book.

Introduction

Lone, wild, and strange, he stood alike exempt
From all affection and from all contempt.
—Byron

The project of this book is to gaze, steadily and attentively, at the deep pool of emotions that converge on one point: longing. When we long, we encounter our own absence. Rilke imagines this aching state: my life without me. This flight from immediacy takes us swiftly elsewhere—to pure intensity, to abandon, to, irrevocably, the other. The gesture of desire, of yearning, is one of surrender; it grasps nothingness greedily. But it also makes nothingness its power; it says "here I am: empty." Yearning lives the emptiness at the back of being: it points to the essential openness at the heart of existence.

Standing always under the sign of longing is the dangerous lover—the one whose eroticism lies in his dark past, his restless inquietude, his remorseful and rebellious exile from comfortable everyday living. His ubiquity marks him as always central to what we mean when we talk about existence and the modern self. And this is not *despite* the fact that he lives and moves and has his being today in popular historical romances and romantic cinema—female-coded genres—but rather *because of* this lowbrow presence. Or, more essentially, because of his lasting and pervasive presence everywhere: he stretches his pained existence back to Elizabethan and Jacobean tragedy and forward to the mass-market romance and to, well, all points in between. Why do we desire so readily, so uninterruptedly and incessantly, the demon lover? Why is it that the subject who lives imprisoned in the blighted landscape of his own mind, who is doomed only to repetition and a desire for death until his possible redemption by the utterly unique moment of love, becomes himself the true cipher of longing, the essence of the movement of desire?

Curiously, the romance with the dark, estranged antihero at its heart—or, what I have named the dangerous lover romance—has not yet been recognized as a distinct genre; it has not been given a history, or shaped into a particular constellation of ideas. While numerous scholars such as Pamela Regis, Catherine Belsey, and Anne Humpherys have discussed specific literary villain/heroes as lovers and their place in particular narratives, there has not been a full-blown exploration of this two-hundred-year cultural phenomenon and its location in both canonized and popular culture. Why is this? Why does the enemy/lover stand on the margins of literary history, waiting to be fully seen? The dangerous lover's obscured, nocturnal location in literary history and his heretofore secret circle of influence fits well with his character; he figures into history on the side of silence, obscurity, nonknowledge, and temporal interruption, rather than on continuity and teleology. But still one must wonder at the paucity of scholarship on a figure that represents a whole radiating nexus of vitally important historical and theoretical issues, including a substantial influence on modern understanding of subject formation. In these times, when Kafka's characters sit and delay, interminably, the decision to *be;* when Hamlet restlessly falls to brooding while the world comes apart around him; when Eliot's hollow men bonelessly look always away, never *at;* failure becomes a constitutive part of ontology. We fail, we are flawed, therefore we are. Now, "when in the restlessness of the interminable and the stagnation of endless error we have to dwell outside of ourselves, outside of the world, and, it would seem, even outside of death" (*Space of Literature,* 159), the dangerous lover steps in, *just here,* and makes the failure at the heart of our being erotic. Our hero tells us that the dangerousness of existence itself must be suffered. The forest is dark and in order to penetrate deeper, one must exile oneself, one must live the Kantian wound—the rupture between interiority and everything exterior. The dangerous lover—the Byronic hero—becomes an emblem of the hero who ventures out into the anguished world in order to find, paradoxically, the self. He moves through the stages of the Hegelian dialectic and, with him, it will often break down, floating him off to the disquietude of the transcendentally homeless.

The dangerous lover romance lends its voice to the buzz of existential questioning. Indeed, it is not too much to say that the forces at work in the attraction to the dangerous lover mirror basic ontological structures. Heidegger's proximity theory particularly exposes the long-standing but secret dialogue between romance and philosophy and explains succinctly the enduring quality of dangerous lover narratives. Heidegger describes being as a process of misunderstanding the authentic self. Caught up in an everyday world of all that appears closest and most familiar to us, we believe that our existence can be explained by what we know well. But ontologically, our most authentic selves lie in what is most mysterious and strange—what appears to be furthest from us. Confronted with authentic being, we feel a sense of terror in the face of the unknown. The dangerous lover narrative makes the same argument about ontology—that our "true" selves reside in what is most strange and enemy-like, in the dangerous other. Related closely to Heidegger's proximity theory is our "being-toward-death"—that our lives can be understood only in relation to our end. The end of the romance transforms love into a possibility, into divine immediacy. Unfolding in the midst of stumbling error, unheard whispers, achingly misunderstood gestures, painful secrets bursting to be exposed, comes a day of grace. The romance story speaks always in relation to the full immanence of love which reaches its culmination at the end of the narrative.[1]

The process of such a love has its uncanny qualities, and it is to the dangerous lover figure we must look in order to find a full embodiment of both Heidegger's and Freud's renderings of uncanniness. The romance heroine finds her most authentic self at the heart of what seems at first most foreign and outside her way of being—an arrogant, hateful other. Romance moves always toward discovery and approaching the impenetrable: what is uncovered is authentic existence in the uncanny other; at the very heart of what appears to be *not* ours comes what we must fully own as ours.

To be attentive to the dangerous lover is to see unfold a new literary history with genealogies of influence that have not yet been properly studied: such as the relationship of the Regency dandy to Victorian Gothic villain/heroes like Rochester, Heathcliff, and Dracula and of the way an amalgam of the gothic and the dandy can be found in various genres of twentieth-century romance. Once one is attuned to the dangerous lover formula, one begins to see it everywhere; the erotic outcast burns brightly through the history of ideas as well as through the history of "trash," the "escapist," the ephemeral. Perennially present, the dangerous lover narrative has become *the* conventional way to represent erotic desire and romantic love. Constructing this fresh literary history discloses contemporary romance's active role as an important producer of cultural meaning, a doubly important recuperative act since female-coded genres are so rarely seen as having this power. The historical trajectory pursued in the following pages is always and everywhere a history of a women's aesthetic—of what women desire, of what turns women on. Thus the following account begins by culling theories of dangerous love from the contemporary romance. With these theories in hand, this itinerary then travels backward to the Gothic, forward through Byron and the nineteenth century. This backwardness underscores the central agenda of this history as a discovery of mythical origins—of the origins of the antihero as he appears today in contemporary romance. Starting with the present and working always in light of this historical or historicist "ending" is a Heideggerian approach to history; he believes that to understand being, one must start from the death of this being and look back, rather than understanding ontology through origins, or beginnings. The strange chronology of the following account is also compelled by the convoluted temporality of the dangerous lover, whose story begins after the damning events of his past have already occurred; hence, in a certain way, his narrative occurs after it has ended.

Dangerous lovers flash out of the general fabric of history writing; by their very radiance they are always exemplary rather than representative. Thus the following exploration treats only of the exemplary, not of the comprehensive, the general, the complete story of every subjectivity with dangerousness in his/her make-up. All history and genre-making is made to be undermined by pointing to subterranean, marginalized, "othered" histories. Seeking to articulate a particular type of longing, bounded large-ly by a women's aesthetic, the following work is limited to male dangerous lovers. A lively history could and must be written on female dangerous lovers, which would take into account the female characters of Keats, Shelley, Coleridge, and Victorian Sensation fiction, among many others.[2]

An essential point of this work is in its stance—it approaches danger-ous subjectivity from a traditional philosophical framework rather than a feminist one.[3] *Not* carefully placing its subject texts within gendered para-digms and a whole host of situational and historical specifics, this study instead treats all the texts under discussion—including canonical, popu-lar, philosophical, and theoretical texts—as equally legitimate and as exist-ing on the same textual plane. By its very nature, philosophy declares that its ideas and experiences apply to everyone, no matter one's situation in place or time, one's positioning in light of gender or race. Why shouldn't the headiness of this powerful dictation of all human experience inform scholarly readings of female-coded formula genres such as the popular romance? They seem never to do so. Does women's desire speak to ques-tions of desire itself—of what it means to devote one's being to yearning? Of course. This is the following study's work: not to read romance using ideas culled from philosophy, but rather to read romance in the same rar-efied light as philosophy in order to discover what romance has to say about the mystery of existence.

CHAPTER ONE

The Erotics of Ontology

The Mass-Market Erotic Historical Romance and Heideggerian Failed Presence (1921–2003)

And so, by a strange and melancholy paradox, the moment of failure is the moment of value; the comprehending and experiencing of life's refusals is the source from which the fullness of life seems to flow. What is depicted is the total absence of any fulfillment of meaning, yet the work attains the rich and rounded fullness of a true totality of life.

—Georg Lukács

I. The Twentieth-Century History of the Erotic Historical Romance, the Gothic Romance, and the Regency Romance

Following the meanderings of the dangerous lover—an etherealized, permeable subjectivity—through the endless generic categories of the contemporary mass-market romance can become a complex task. But for such a task to be undertaken, we must find a way to categorize, classify, and differentiate genres in the interest of literary-history making. The heterogeneity of the market and the fact that publishers, following buying trends, have little need to keep to any system of regularized labeling or of accurate descriptions of the generic category of their products make taxonomic rubrics problematic. Romance historians have shaped this heterogeneity in various ways; two obvious rubrics are the contemporary and the historical romance which refer to a whole host of differences, not only that of a modern or a past setting.[1] Within these categories two others become helpful—the "sweet," a more traditional narrative with little to no sexual explicitness, or the "erotic," soft to hardcore porn, sometimes with sadomasochistic elements.

The dangerous lover lurks in almost all the categories of romance. Yet there is one type that seems almost antithetic to his nature as the outsider hero, as the unrevealed stranger with his potential or actual violence: the "erotic" contemporary. In fact, both hero and heroine in this type are enmeshed in an active, open, workaday world, presented in a contemporary setting. The "New Hero," as Thurston calls him, comes onto the scene as a man whose kindness, generosity, easygoing even-temperedness attracts the heroine, who is often initially more interested in her career than in marriage and a man.[2] Harlequin describes the latter line to potential writers as containing "emotional and sensual content supported by a sense of community" (Harlequin Web site). The erotic contemporary romance sets itself apart from the dangerous lover kind in its focus on bringing the lovers into life among people, into a friendly love that lives in an everyday world. Their love takes them deeper into the societal fold, into developed connections with the community, into a safe, accepted union. This is not the world of the dangerous lover.

In her study of early romance genres (from 1674 to 1740), Ros Ballaster creates two categories of use here: didactic love fiction and amatory fiction. For Ballaster, the amatory fiction of Aphra Behn, Delariviere Manley, and Eliza Haywood is the early modern equivalent of the contemporary mass-market romance. The erotic contemporary romance falls under Ballaster's category of didactic love fiction—romance that has a didactic project, is future-directed, and attempts to represent a moral way of living, a "just" kind of love (depending on what constitutes the "morals" of the particular time period in question). On the opposite extreme, the dangerous lover type falls under the rubric of amatory fiction. Amatory fiction cannot be, generally speaking, recuperated morally, nor does it play out in a socially sanctioned realm. The anarchical rebelliousness of the dangerous lover narrative—its moments of frozen inarticulateness—undercut a didactic project. In its aestheticization of failure, dangerous love has its foundations in the finitude of being, on the edge of silence, in fragmentation, and in disintegration. Dangerous love plays with the outside—of possibility, life in society, happiness. The dangerous beloved hides a secret melancholy interiority that flashes out in passionate violence and rage. His misanthropy and self-exiled otherness cover a nature that once believed so deeply in ideals such as Truth, Beauty, and Purity, that his fall from this grace of faith plunges him into a doom of profoundly embittered brooding. The dangerous lover actively maintains and embraces his failure by his work to remain outside social approval and morals.

Erotic outsiders also make their mark in "sweet" ("old-fashioned") romances, of the contemporary sort as well as the historical type. Associated primarily with Harlequin's series, the "sweet" romance genre or category books (also called "brand-name" romances) play a surprisingly seminal role in the study of romance itself because many theorists of the mass-market romance conflate all romance genres and call them

"Harlequins." Such a conflation boils a complex constellation of genres down to one simple plot and one single publisher of this plot. Tania Modleski is one such theorist: all mass-market romances, to her, are "Harlequins." She writes that,

> . . . the formula rarely varies: a young, inexperienced, poor to moderately well-to-do woman encounters and becomes involved with a handsome, strong, experienced, wealthy man, older than herself by ten to fifteen years. The heroine is confused by the hero's behaviour since, though he is obviously interested in her, he is mocking, cynical, contemptuous, often hostile, and even somewhat brutal. By the end, however, all misunderstandings are cleared away, and the hero reveals his love for the heroine, who reciprocates. (35–36)

A real simplification happens here: Modleski sees only one type of romance where there is a great heterogeneity. But it is hard not to see that this essentializing has much truth to it as well: the above sketch presents the skeletal structure of most dangerous lover plots. Yet it does miss out entirely on the erotic contemporary romance as described above, and it presents the erotic historical romance with all its excesses removed.

As the above quotation lays bare, the "sweet" romance contains the enemy lover. Contrary to all expectation, the dangerous subject appears in this form of didactic fiction. As we move back into our history, we will see this construction again and again: the hero set up as dangerous only to then be reformed in the end, brought from the outside into the domestic life of the heterosexual couple. While he is yet our outsider hero, the "sweet" dangerous lover does not carry with him the roiling interior, the barely suppressed fury, the radical darkness of the hero of the "erotic" historical. This brings us to the other important classification of romances: the historical romance. Under this rubric fall "erotic" historicals, as well as the "regency" romance, the historical "sweet" romance, and the modern gothic romance. The historicals overflow with erotic outcasts of various types and intensities: here he rises in all his multifoliate splendor. Not only that: the historicals are links in a solid literary-historical chain, stretching back into the dark reaches of the past. Their heterogeneity can be described with Ballaster's categories: "erotic" historicals are purely amatory fiction, and the gothic, the regency, and the historical "sweet" are varying mixtures of amatory and didactic fiction.

It is with the historicals that the history of the dangerous lover unfolds into the present hour. Opening the pulpy pages of the fat erotic historical romance novel, we find the most salient and loud representation of the dangerous lover narrative: the hero's rough, mysterious strangeness and his present clouded by a dark past and unreadable emotions unfold in settings distant in time and place, large in historical sweep. The exoticism of the historical romance sets an air of unfamiliarity around the whole narrative, lending the proper atmosphere for a figure out of fantasy, with the nebulous characterization of an archetype.

The dangerous lover steps out of a mythical realm; his construction from an archetypal past maintains its saliency, no matter how real his person. His subjectivity stretches back through time to other mythical figures. As each age remakes myth in its image, the dangerous lover opens out of the uncertainty of the historically great; his dangerousness lies in the unknowability of the past itself, particularly the past of myth. His dangerousness is located in fantasy, in ways that his subjectivity is not representative of some concrete reality, but in changeability, imagination, reformulation. On some level the dangerous lover hides in myth; he retreats from present being into being an other from the past. And to love a dangerous lover is also to step into the fantasy of mythology and its truth, seemingly frozen yet always shifting. To retreat into myth is to step out of the present and re-create a past, larger than life. Barthes writes of this desire for the "impenetrable object" of the other, for the other who is "not to be known": "I am then seized with that exaltation of loving someone unknown, someone who will remain so forever: a mystic impulse: I know what I do not know" (*Lover's Discourse,* 135).

In the erotic historical, dramatic upheavals give the dangerous lover and the heroine permission to be involved in extreme adventures, violent encounters, tense battles. The dangerous lover may be a pirate like Captain Marques, a "battered slave of the world" (108) as he calls himself, who kidnaps the heroine in Elizabeth Doyle's *My Lady Pirate;* or Stone McBride, a ruthless rancher, quarreling irreconcilably with his family, lost to his true love, hence entirely outcast and even uncaring of his fate, in Evelyn Rogers's *The Loner;* or the disinherited bastard of an English lord, seeking revenge for his father's rejection of him, who is now a "flinty" gambling casino owner who forces the heroine to marry him to escape penury, as in Barbara Dawson Smith's *Seduced by a Scoundrel.* Or he may be the wandering cowboy like Kain Debolt in *Winds of Promise:* "He was a loner, making a few friends here and there, but never settling in one place long enough to establish roots. Now he wondered at the emptiness of his life" (60).[3]

The rough-hewn excess of the erotic historical romance (sometimes called the "bodice ripper," "slave narrative," or "sweet savage" romance and one of the most sexually explicit of the romance genres) can be immediately located in its representation of sexual extremity: the innocent heroines, usually virgins, are roughly seduced, perhaps even raped, by much older, more experienced heroes. The power differential between the hero and heroine and his violent control over her drives the plot, which is essentially a slow movement of power passing from the hero to the heroine. Despite her initial distressing vulnerability, bodily weakness, and real inexperience of the world and all its dangers, or perhaps because of it, at the end of the novel the hero grovels at her feet. Modleski argues that this is one of the functions of romance, a kind of revenge fantasy where the haughty hero is brought to heel: "all the while he is being so hateful, he is internally groveling, groveling, groveling" (45). His enraptured and abandoned love for her becomes a dependence on her love so excessive that she not only has him utterly in her power, but she takes on many of his mesmerizing and erotic characteristics—a manifold subjectivity, a mysterious past—and even develops a heroic independence through the adventures recounted in the narrative. She obtains a shadowy, perhaps even dark side through the hero's amorous witnessing of her erotic depths. She will often withdraw from society with the outcast dangerous lover, and their extreme investment in the couple serves to further alienate them from others.

The hero of the erotic historical can be compared to that famous writer of failure—Kafka. Walter Benjamin writes of Kafka's sense of failure: "One is tempted to say: once he was certain of eventual failure, everything worked out for him en route as in a dream" (*Illuminations,* 144). The hero of the erotic historical has already fallen into error at the beginning of the narrative; he begins with a subjectivity so deeply desiring, so impossible to satiate, his desires are left wanting. His very mistakes are powerful forces because they bring with them the mastery of despair, torment—the possibility of failure as large as the world. Because of the endlessly expansive nature of his desires, his power is world-encompassing: he can decimate the whole world with the scowl on his face. His seductiveness can be located here: the one who loves him can grasp the power of impossibility; she can make the world possible by being, herself, the plenitude, the immanent meaning of existence for him. The hero's belief in his brilliance, his superior, misanthropic position above all others and their run-of-the-mill lives, is so very believable to the heroine that to change this decimation to plenitude becomes her reason for being. To believe in the dangerous lover is to be drawn to him with the ties of despair and failure, to feel that oneself also fails, and success comes out of the center of this final despair.

Legend has it that the erotic historical sprang, full-grown and kicking, out of the head of Kathleen Woodiwiss and stormed brazenly onto the romance novel scene. Between 1972 and 1974 romance sales were down, publishers were looking for a new formula, and Nancy Coffey of Avon books discovered Woodiwiss's *The Flame and the Flower* (1972) from a stack of unsolicited manuscripts. Longer than other romances then on the market, its sexual encounters were more graphic and violent and there was a grandness of design, involving extensive travel and high adventure, heretofore unseen. The sweeping popularity of this new formula electrified the whole market; hundreds of thousands of romance lovers became burningly obsessed.[4] Soon after Woodiwiss's resounding success Avon came out with Rosemary Rogers's *Sweet Savage Love* (1974), giving the new formula one of its names: the "sweet savage" romance. What was it about the "bodice-ripper" that caused such a historical break, a radical shift in romance formulas thereafter? Their essential charm stems from their erotic dangerousness, their near-pornographic sexual violence, and their eroticization of travel, of the world and all its exhilarating experiences. In fact, experience itself becomes erotically dangerous, a sublime reaching toward transcendence, or a final movement toward a heroic and ecstatic death. The formula hinges on the elusive and cryptic hero who gestures toward the endless possibility of erotic darkness.

Brandon, the hero of *The Flame and the Flower,* emanates ominous blackness: hair that is "raven black," skin that is "darkly tanned"; he "sweeps" the heroine "with a bold gaze from top to toe" (31). His desires turn on cruel mastery and imprisonment of the heroine; his evil actions set him apart from earlier mass-market formulas as a character singularly unredeemable: "He had the look of a pirate about him, or even Satan himself" (31). "Tall and powerful he stood, garmented regally in black velvet and flawless white. He was Satan to her. Handsome. Ruthless. Evil. He could draw her soul from her body and never feel remorse" (92). The erotic fantasy of being subjugated—terrified and trembling—by such an archetypal enemy figure hinges, once again, on *his* subjugation at the end of the novel by his love for the heroine. He tumbles from masterful demon lover to having a body that is pale, that trembles, mirroring her physical terror upon first meeting him. "The breath caught in Brandon's throat. He went pale and suddenly began to shake. He cursed himself for letting a mere girl affect him this way. She played havoc with his insides. He felt as if he were again a virgin, about to experience his first woman. He was hot and sweating one moment, cold and shaking another" (152).[5] Tossed from one passionate, self-decimating extreme to another, the hero of the erotic historical embodies a grandness of contradiction distinct from other romance formulas, particularly earlier ones, and his dramatic transformation from distant, cold villain to burning lover whose world resides in the heroine is more violently exaggerated than in any other romance genre. It is this excessiveness that pulls the erotic historical toward the genre of pornography. Both genres tend to repeat again and again the point of supersaturation of meaning—with pornography this point is penetration, and with the erotic historical it is the passionate frisson between the hero and heroine.

Steve Morgan, the hero of *Sweet Savage Love,* cynical gunfighter, ever-wandering killer, is so full of dark experience and secret doings that his past is never finally told and resolved. Steve's life as a homeless fighter does not change with his final transformation into a lover; he takes the heroine along with him on his travels, and she herself becomes a vagabond and fugitive. In the erotic historical, distinct from other contemporary mass-markets, the lovers remain outside, wayfarers on the margins of society. In all the heroes of this genre, we find something of Rhett Butler from Margaret Mitchell's *Gone with the Wind* (1936) (itself an early classic of the erotic historical genre). A perennial influence on enemy lovers everywhere, Rhett introduces us to the cynical libertine who hides an interior of deep disappointment. He self-destructively gestures again and again to his fall-enness, goading society to cast him out more and more: "Suppose I don't want to redeem myself?" Rhett asks. "Why should I fight to uphold the system that cast me out? I shall take pleasure in seeing it smashed" (240). A ruined idealist, he has before him a world void of real truth, of strong principle and moral rectitude; thus he tumbles into the abyss with an unimaginable grace and charm.

Rhett presents us with that common twist on the erotic outcast char-acter: the dandy. He wears "the clothes of a dandy on a body that was powerful and latently dangerous in its lazy grace" (179). We often encounter the dandified dangerous lover, as we see with Oscar Wilde's characters (and Wilde himself and his fellow Aesthetes), the Byronic hero in the popular imagination (and Byron himself), and many characters from contemporary romances (particularly the erotic historical and the regency genres). This performance of eccentricity, showiness, and bold statement expresses a sense of mastery over social codes and gestures—a mastery to the point of deconstructing them. Exaggerating such social expressions performs an ironic disenchantment and, to reference stock Romantic ideas, a sense of self so singular that, even visibly, he "stands out." To "stand out," though, asks for witnesses to self-exile; the danger-ous lover "confesses" his disappointment in a world too shallow for him; his only recourse is to parody this lack of soul. To be superficial on the surface is to point to and, at the same time, hide an interior. Confession is eroticized with dangerous subjectivity: the secret depth of the soul is unveiled to the beloved and the beloved only, and when it's exposed the fact that it can't be represented is uncovered. Such is the paradox; the lover says: "Here is the depth of my pain, see how it can never be understood."

Yet the dangerous lover's infinite subjectivity is infinite only insofar as it is confessed and witnessed—its very presentation guarantees its unrepresentability. As Barthes affirms of the lover: " . . . passion is in essence made to be seen: the hiding must be seen: I want you to know that I am hiding something from you, that is the active paradox I must resolve: at one and the same time it must be known and not known" (*Lover's Discourse,* 42). What the dandy expresses with his style is that his style can never represent him.

While Rhett is a rascal, when he loves he is the best of men, but he must hide this because, more than any other man, he feels he has failed on a grand scale. Maintaining complete indifference for the world and in the world is essential, otherwise his hell will cut deeper, his lacerated interiority will be exposed to further wounding. The world mirrors his subjectivity: a lost cause. Only the heroine witnesses his depths of strength and hence also the depths of his final despair. All others see only his reckless, insolent façade. With Rhett we are reminded of the self emptied or the absence of being—his eroticism sets before us our own death, our own darkness. Scarlett describes her first encounter with this erotic: "He was like death, carrying her away in arms that hurt. . . . She was darkness and he was darkness and there had never been anything before this time, only darkness and his lips upon hers. . . . Suddenly she had a wild thrill like she had never known; joy, fear, madness, excitement" (940). Barthes writes of this craving to be engulfed or annihilated as part of the lover's discourse. It is a dying without the pains of dying, "the gentleness of the abyss" (11) where responsibility no longer holds one in its clutches.

The beauty of erotic death is replayed in another classic dangerous lover narrative, as well as an early and influential erotic historical—Edith M. Hull's *The Sheik* (1921), considered by some to be the first romance of the twentieth century.[6] The sheik of the title kidnaps, rapes, and holds captive an aristocratic English girl.[7] Again the inexorable divide: the mysterious, ruthless leader of a roving band of Arabs and the subjugated, enslaved English girl. The sheik has "the handsomest and cruelest face that she had ever seen. . . . He was looking at her with fierce burning eyes that swept her until she felt that the boyish clothes that covered her slender limbs were stripped from her" (56–57). She observes that " . . . his face was the face of a devil" (141). His subjectivity has the hiddenness of danger: "The man himself was a mystery. . . . She could not reconcile him and . . . [the] dozen incongruities that she had noticed during the day crowded into her recollection until her head reeled"(79). He has exiled himself from his aristocratic English origins; he wanders the desert incessantly. Redemption from self-inflicted loneliness comes finally through true love. His only escape must be from outside, through a transcendence which he can't possibly see beforehand because it is so exterior to any kind of solution he could find for himself. The lover brings the caesura, the utter surprise of an interruption of restless being. As an outsider love narrative, *The Sheik* ends with the declaration of love signifying a pact to wander together as homeless voyagers.

The Sheik makes fast the chain that links the erotic historical with pornography (and we will see everywhere these links between the dangerous lover romance and pornography, particularly in the nineteenth century). Even though Hull's story is not sexually explicit—in fact, on the page we only read about kisses—she rewrites and romanticizes a popular nineteenth-century pornographic narrative.[8] The darling of nineteenth-century pornographers, the story of an exotic foreigner—a Turk, a sheik, a pirate, a brigand—enslaving and raping a pale and supplicant English virgin provided the ultimate titillation for the English gentleman reader. The anonymous *The Lustful Turk: Scenes in the Harem of an Eastern Potentate,* published around 1828, provides us with a famous example of a pornographic version of *The Sheik.* The narrative of *The Lustful Turk,* up until the all-important ending, is essentially the same as the sheik romance. Of course, with the romance the ending is everything: in *The Sheik,* the transcendent sphere of love "redeems" the brutality of the hero, casting a rosy glow of forever back on all sadistic acts. The pornographic version merely repeats, unrelentingly, the act of penetration, of possession. No transcendence here: meaning flattens out into a repetition which could sustain itself forever.[9]

A writer and theorist who brings together this heady constellation of ideas—love as redemptive, sadomasochistic sexuality as transcendent, death as erotic—and who was writing around the same time as Hull comes into the history of the dangerous lover just here: D. H. Lawrence. His novels abound with demon lovers who "save" women from the social order; his stories explore time and again the tie between sex and death, the *liebestod;* and his descriptions of sexual and spiritual union provide a high-brow and mythical prototype for the scenes of transcendence in the erotic historical. As a didactic essayist Lawrence locates spirituality exclusively in the act of romantic love. In his essay entitled "Love," the coupling of two people provides the only type of grace achievable in this world. Love, here, holds the same kind of power of transcendental sublimity as in all true romance; in fact, Lawrence's theories on love and sexuality provided a prototype for romance writers, particularly the model of *Lady Chatterley's Lover.* Lawrence describes love as "neither temporal nor spiritual but absolved by the equality of perfection, pure immanence of absolution" (*Sex,* 35). The essence of love, for Lawrence, resides in its very incompletion: "But if all be united in one bond of love, then there is no more love. And, therefore, for those who are in love with love, to travel is better than to arrive. For in arriving one passes beyond love, or rather, one encompasses love in a new transcendence. . . . Love is not a goal; it is only traveling" (*Sex,* 33–34). The near/far that love requires is similarly structured as the "nearness" of hero and heroine throughout the erotic historical narrative: the desire that always needs distance to be kept alive. Love and travel become intricately connected, describing the large-as-the-world quality of outsider lovers.[10]

Gerald in *Women in Love* (1920)—one of the clearest dangerous lover figures in Lawrence—stands in Lawrence's visionary, prophetic universe as the moribund wrestler with his soul who is finally dominated by dissolution and disintegration. A lover who represents the isolation and desolation bred by the modern age, Gerald's self defines a microcosm of chaos: " . . . life was a hollow shell all round him, roaring and clattering like the sound of the sea . . . and inside this hollow shell was all the darkness and fearful space of death . . . he would collapse inwards upon the great dark void which circled at the center of his soul" (314–15). Cain-like, Gerald shotguns his brother and his family is cursed mysteriously: "There's one thing about our family, you know. Once anything goes wrong, it can never be put right again" (176). Erotic outcasts descend from Cain in their isolation, searching, restlessness, sense of living always in a cursed state, and self-made tragedies. Gerald's subjectivity, almost redeemed by his lover, Gudrun, finally collapses in on its own hell. His existential despair as a Modernist hero mirrors the blighted heroes of the erotic historical yet without the final transformation: erotic outcasts in romance are created to be absolved and filled by love.

Gerald's erotic sadism mesmerizes Gudrun; the sight of him overmastering his horse purely for pleasure brings intense sexual longing:

> Gudrun was as if numbed in her mind by the sense of indomitable
> soft weight of the man, bearing down into the living body of the
> horse: the strong, indomitable thighs of the blond man clenching
> the palpitating body of the mare into pure control; a sort of soft
> white magnetic domination from the loins and thighs and calfs,
> enclosing and encompassing the mare heavily into unutterable sub-
> ordination, soft-blooded subordination, terrible. (106)

The erotic power of Gerald and Gundrun together has a dark potency, an "underworld knowledge": "through her passion was a transcendent fear of the thing he was . . . oh, how dangerous! . . . such an unutterable enemy" (324). Her longing for erotic annihilation does not bring ultimate transcendence as such yearnings do in the romance. The sadomasochistic erotic of Lawrence, divorced from the transcendent discourse of the romance, often becomes his means for pointing to the cruel emptiness of the modern world itself, and, unlike the author of the romance novel, Lawrence sometimes feels compelled to moralize against this attraction to death. Yet Lawrence further complicates and clouds the picture by setting up erotic longing for death as possibly a site for elemental regeneration. With both couples of *Women in Love*—Gerald and Gundrun, and Ursula and Birkin—we find an occasional desire to kill the beloved which Lawrence casts as a desire "natural" to the primitive animalism of human sexuality.[11] Sex often becomes a satisfying way of dissolving the other and annihilating the self, and such a communing with the basic needs of our natures might bring an illumination of being, a clearing out of space amid the chaos and emptiness. Lawrence is the writer we look to when we want to try to understand the terror of love, the utter nightmare of coming close to the other.

The classic Lawrencian meditation on the ecstatic powers of the awakened erotic is *Lady Chatterley's Lover* (1928). Mellors, Lady Chatterley's working-class demon lover, an outsider type who should now be familiar to us, is the "strange and terrible" other whose cosmic unknownness causes her to "dare to let go everything, all herself" (260). Out of his misanthropic search for the "bitter privacy of a man who at last wants to be alone" (166), Mellors finds sexual conflagration and spiritual absolution with Lady Chatterley. Their eroticism makes the world strange again; it throws a light on the true oddness of existence. Albeit in a somewhat different register, sex scenes in the erotic historical mimic Lawrence's famous descriptions of sex as world changing, world swaying, as a door to a mysticism that seeks to explain everything. Like the heroines of the erotic historical, Lady Chatterley's sexual awakening brings with it a kind of erotic religious faith:

> And now she touched him, and it was the sons of gods with the daughters of men. How beautiful he felt, how pure in tissue! . . . Beauty! What beauty! A sudden little flame of new awareness went through her. . . . And the strange weight of the balls between his legs! What a mystery! What a strange heavy weight of mystery that could lie soft and heavy in one's hand! The roots, root of all that is lovely, the primeval root of all full beauty. . . . She could not know what it was. She could not remember what it had been. . . . And afterwards she was utterly still, utterly unknowing, she was not aware for how long. (263)

Her unrestrained movement of abandon brings her to the favorable hour of divine immediacy.

Lawrence eroticizes failure by making love and sex a part of the heady mix of Modernist agonies: using sexuality he describes both the move toward and away from the alienated emptiness of subjectivity. Lawrence brought pornography into a narrative of existential angst and spiritual transcendence, a move essential to the erotic historical's development both as a more sexually explicit medium and as a narrative of love as spiritually redemptive.

The erotic historical grows out of the older genre of the gothic romance like a new shoot emerging from the same tree. In fact, all contemporary romance seems to grow out of the gothic: many of its dark and secret themes still resonate. On a very small scale, the gothic also maintains its status as a genre existing side by side with the others. While only one true gothic romance line still exists—Dorchester's gothic "Candleglow" series—the popularity of the gothic romance is slowly being revivified, along with the resurgence of all things gothic: the pallor; the morbid sensibility; the whited, undead sepulcher; the haunted interior.[12] A certain postfeminist climate has been an important factor in the return of this genre of romance. Postfeminism, while recognizing the advances of the feminists that have come before it, loosens some of the tight holds of early feminism and is willing to reappropriate certain paradigms that were earlier deemed dangerous to feminism, such as the attraction of the demon lover.[13]

In regards to the demon lover, we must pay particular attention here to the hero of the twentieth-century gothic romance and the way that he manages to embody two stock characters that appear earlier as two opposite extremes: the virtuous, courtly hero and the debased, sullied villain. And in this lies the primary difference between the twentieth-century gothic romance and the late-eighteenth-century, early-nineteenth-century Gothic proper: the conflation in the twentieth century of the enemy/lover into one character. David Richter points to this masterful intertwining of characteristics when he argues that the Gothic novel (1780s–1820s) is essentially a failed genre and that it only found its mode of coherence after the end of its popularity. The Gothic novel's confusion lay in the distinct moral opposites of the two flat, one-dimensional characters of the good and the bad man; success came only with the Brontës' reinscription of the hero/villain as one character, the "threat and reward" (Richter, 106) combined in one man. Sin and guilt, two expressions of subjectivity in the Gothic, reach the closure of redemption in love in *Jane Eyre* or the spectral transcendence of love as freedom after death in *Wuthering Heights*.

The heroine of Phyllis Whitney's *Thunder Heights* (1960), one of the first of the new gothics, receives a summons from her rich uncle from whom she has been estranged due to an old family quarrel, and she finds herself inheriting a huge gothic mansion inhabited by her relations.[14] The house holds many threatening secrets (a requirement for the genre), and Camilla fears for her life. The hero, Ross Granger, worked as a consultant for her now-dead uncle and still lives in the house. Because of his sometimes shadowy manner, she believes he may be the one making attempts on her life, but finds the culprit is actually her aunt's adopted son, Booth Hendricks, who she discovers also killed her mother. The heroine experiences erotic tensions with both men, and both of them, at various points, hold the role of dangerous lover. Characteristically, it is Booth, the truly threatening of the two, who maintains the strongest erotic pull. Both men contain hidden sadnesses; their glances are angry and they lurk about, spying on the heroine. But of Booth she asks herself: "What haunted this man? What drove him and made him so strange? Darkly strange and strangely fascinating" (94). She "was sharply aware of him close at her side, moving with his air of restrained vitality, as though the dark power that flowed through him was held for the moment in leash . . . he filled her with a sense of—was it attraction or alarm? Perhaps a mingling of both, for it might be dangerous to grow too interested in this man" (96). But Ross, the less developed of the two characters, saves her from Booth and from her attraction to him; all of his mysterious ways magically fall away and he becomes her true haven.

Camilla's wondering over the spectrality of Booth's thoughts points to the ways the dangerous lover is continually haunted by an other self—one who has not been schooled in disappointment, one who loves in a just world where he is accepted and accepting, one whose desires can be fulfilled, his ideals made real. The haunting past self, always too late to *be*, has never been alive. This spectrality is one of the keys to the way the contemporary dangerous lover comes out of the Gothic villain. His lover, his redemption, creates another kind of haunting: she is the specter of those lost ideals, those profound desires never to be fulfilled. Her insubstantiality comes from her relation to him as an impossibility. Their togetherness, an embodiment of all his desires, can only happen on the level of a haunting, a fragmentary whispering, a groaning, a dreamscape occurring on the margins of sanity, of the everyday real. Numerous erotic historicals describe their heroes, and often even their heroines, as haunted and haunting. "He was a dark looming silhouette over her, and were it not for the feel of his hard body pressing onto hers, she would have thought him a phantom lover" (Becnel, 82). Or, in *Stranger in Paradise* (1995), the hero "looked ghostly in the moonglow, a haunting figure from the nether world" (44). The outsider demon lover's flash of presence, which happens in an impossible moment of spectral being, does not, cannot, have the substantiality of people who love and live, who work in societal duty. Their presence together, haunted always by impoverished being, by the loss of being nonexistent, creates dark, nonluminous figures whose lives are already extinguished. In *Wed to a Stranger?* (1997), the lovers have "a relationship of shadows—forged from veiled half truths and illusions" (172). In some sense the dangerous lover has already ended his life when the narrative begins; he has fallen, failed, been cast out, lost everything. His story of love then happens in an afterlife, a dark fairy tale of no possibility.

In non-gothic twentieth-century romance (and especially in the erotic historical) traces of the original mechanisms can be discovered, such as the bifurcated, schizophrenic hero. In Julie McBride's *Wed to a Stranger?* the hero doubles himself, with Jekyll and Hyde flair. After her husband mysteriously disappears, Fritzi is stalked by a dashing man who flits into her house at night to watch her sleep. This second man turns out to be her husband, who she discovers is a plastic surgeon working for a government antiterrorist unit. His face, altered by plastic surgery when he married her, is altered back after his disappearance. Not surprisingly, he is now more devastatingly handsome with a dark and powerful presence and, rather than being a dangerous stalker, has all along been protecting her. The gothic double represents, in a sometimes simplistic and clunky manner, the deep mystery of the unconscious, the way that the other, who seems like a unified, integral subjectivity, can suddenly become a stranger, as if a mask has fallen away and revealed an endless series of masks. The comfort of the romance lies in the cessation of the dizzying layers, the reaching of one true self who is the perfect beloved, never to change, never to stop loving.

Two classics of the twentieth-century gothic genre—and their types of the enemy/lover—take us immediately back to that ur-gothic romance: *Jane Eyre*. Du Maurier's Max de Winter (*Rebecca*) is Rochester revivified and Victoria Holt's Connan TreMellyn (*Mistress of Mellyn*, 1960) replicates to perfection Max de Winter. Striking similarities in plot structure solidify the historical chain of influence: the seemingly or actually haunted mansion; the dead and/or imprisoned previous wife; the young and plain governess/companion, orphaned, forlorn; the marriage proposal that is suspect, unreal, yet so welcome.[15] The heroines of these three novels vary greatly, the clearest example being Jane's self-willed determination compared to *Rebecca's* heroine's lack of self-esteem and constant ontological instability. Yet they all desire, as Jane describes, to plumb the hero's abyssal subjectivity, to discern, understand, see, his vast mindscape. Jane looks into Rochester's face and eyes,

> . . . and as for the vague something . . . that opened on a careful observer, now and then, in his eye, and closed again before one could fathom the strange depth partially disclosed; that something which used to make me fear and shrink, as if I had been wandering amongst volcanic-looking hills, and had suddenly felt the ground quiver, and seen it gape. . . . Instead of wishing to shun, I longed only to dare—to divine . . . the abyss. (213)

The heroine, and especially the reader, is never able to fully know this abyss. But oddly, and this is one of the many irresolvable paradoxes of the dangerous lover, Connan, Max, and Rochester, while represented as infinite, often don't have much depth to plumb.[16] Writing on Byron, Andrew Elfenbein argues that the seeming depth of these infinite Romantic subjectivities actually uncovers the possibility of exhausting these depths easily. Passions so deep that they are obscured and thus not representable could easily be read as lacking altogether. The dangerous lover has a "subjectivity perpetually at risk" (*Byron,* 28), and his fragility is expressed by the need for a repetition of this character, in romance after romance. Romances need to, again and again, shore up a paradigm whose existence, always only on the surface, requires a continual reiteration. Any epistemology of the surface would have to include the dangerous lover.

Maxim de Winter wears the Cain-like mark, the pained mask: "He will look lost and puzzled suddenly, all expression dying away from his dear face, a sculptured thing, formal and cold, beautiful still but lifeless" (5). Forced restlessly to traverse the world after he thinks he has murdered his first wife, Max becomes another disinherited exile. Even his marriage to the heroine can only temporally redeem him; after the revenant of his murdered wife, Mrs. Danvers, burns down his home, Max and his second wife become estranged from all society. When the heroine first meets him, Max steps out of timeless myth. "His face was arresting, sensitive, medieval in some strange inexplicable way. . . . Could one but rob him of his English tweeds, and put him in black, with lace at his throat and wrists, he would stare down at us in our new world from a long distant past—a past where men walked cloaked at night, and stood in the shadow of old doorways, a past of narrow stairways and dim dungeons, a past of whispers in the dark, of shimmering rapier blades, of silent, exquisite courtesy" (15). Max emerges out of a Gothic past, like a glimmer out of the darkness of history. His mythic proportions create the hiddenness of his interiority; he is " . . . a man of yesterday wrapped in his secret self" (29). Dangerous love often turns time into melancholy loss, and *Rebecca* is suffused with the melancholy of time passing, "Even today, when shutting drawers and flinging wide a hotel wardrobe . . . I am aware of a sense of sadness, of a sense of loss. This has been ours, however brief the time. Though only two nights have been spent beneath a roof, yet we leave something of ourselves behind" (44). These exiled lovers must keep restlessly roving, as if they were searching for something, yet there is nothing for them to find.

In Holt's *Mistress of Mellyn,*[17] Martha Leigh, a plain governess, arrives at an ancient, windswept gothic mansion with secret doors, chambers, peep-holes, and rumors of murder to take on her position as teacher to the young daughter of the master of the house, Connan TreMellyn.[18] Connan's wife recently died under sinister and mysterious circumstances (echoing Rebecca and Bertha), and Martha becomes obsessed with finding out what happened to her, suspecting that she is still living and being held prisoner in the house by Connan or that she was murdered by him and is buried somewhere nearby. Martha finds Connan potently lethal, with a menacing silence and a buried self. "He gave an impression of both strength and cruelty. . . . There was sensuality in that face . . . but there was much else that was hidden" (36). She asks, "Was there a streak of sadism in his nature?" (41). Martha falls for this brooding interiority, and suddenly a strange light flashes out of it: he proposes marriage. Not convinced he really loves her, she is suspicious and wary even while she accepts. His proposal itself has gothic overtones—he "mocks," "I want to marry you because I want to keep you a prisoner in my house" (200). Martha must confront the fact that she "had fallen in love with a murderer" (211). She even makes the decision, "I would rather meet death at his hands than leave him and be forced to endure an empty life without him" (220). But like all gothic romance, the menacing man turns into, first and foremost, a lover: Connan is not the murderer of his wife.

Connan's eroticism comes from his bleak, enigmatic brooding. In contemporary erotic historicals, the hero's depth of thought and ruminations can often be read on his face, by a "small muscle [which] worked furiously in the corner of his jaw, and his lips [which] thinned dangerously" (Jackson, 104). Sometimes his features "tighten," or his eyes become shadowed, darkened, glinting. His pained expression indicates the vastness of his desolated interiority. Rorik, in Catherine Coulter's *Lord of Hawkfell Island* (1993), expresses this profundity of somber self: "He felt as though he were dying, not of wounds valiantly gained, but from deep inside him where there was naught but emptiness and pain and regret and guilt" (208). Or in Dorothy Garlick's *Wind of Promise* (1987), the hero sees himself as "a restless man, seeking to fill an emptiness inside him" (3). Walter Benjamin describes the sadness of the brooder, as opposed to the simple thinker:

> What fundamentally distinguishes the brooder from the thinker is that the former not only meditates a thing but also meditates his meditation of the thing. The case of the brooder is that of the man who has arrived at the solution of a great problem but then has forgotten it. And now he broods—not so much over the matter itself as over his past reflections on it. The brooder's thinking, therefore, bears the imprint of memory. (*Arcades Project*, 367)

The dangerous lover does not brood about the answer, but about having lost it. Hence his brooding is about loss per se, the thinking of loss, and how time sustains it. Brooding creates the impression of a multichambered mind full of layered thoughts complex enough always to leave food for more brooding. The brooder is self-contained; he can entertain himself with his mind, always finding fresh scenes and activities within. If we read the word "brooding" in another sense, we can see the absorbed, not-quite-purposeful subject as feminized, as one who sits over his eggs until their time has come to hatch. The power of the brooder lies in the attraction of his disconsolate independence. Love, however, gives his brooding a witness, a circumscribed reason. The lover acts, caresses, kisses, in an attempt to break in on the brooding of the beloved.

Not only do we find gothic demon lovers in contemporary romance, a certain gothic air settles over much of the literature. Ancient mansions, castles, and keeps draw the heroine, such as the centuries-old Scottish manor house in Haywood Smith's *Border Lord,* where the hero, a villain called the "Black Bastard," holds the heroine prisoner. Imprisonment and rape are also common elements, as we have seen with *The Flame and the Flower.* In *Sweet Savage Love,* the heroine is held captive by the hero, as well as by other villains, and she is raped many times. In *Lord of Danger,* the hero is a magician who lives in a castle. Many of Catherine Coulter's novels contain gothic themes and settings, with heroines often kidnapped, immured in castles, and subject to violence and villainy.

The gothic theme of imprisonment appears in the erotic historical as an ontological state of blocked access. Most importantly, one is closed off from some fundamental aspect of subjectivity. Eve Kosofsky Sedgwick points out that much of the tension of the Gothic comes from the experience of being denied access to a space, literal or metaphorical, and figuring out how to discover a passage between the inside and outside. This could, Sedgwick notes, be the self's own past and family history, a lover, or even simply the free air, when the self is victim of live burial. In these two spaces—within the isolation and within the space out of reach—meaning is held apart from its true completion. In *Mysteries of Udolpho,* Emily, imprisoned in the castle in close proximity to the villain, pines for her lover, Valancourt, who is somewhere outside. She lives with the dangers within, while longing for knowledge about the presence of the lover without. The three primary delineations of this arrangement—what is inside, outside, and what separates them—are repeated again and again in the gothic and the erotic historical and gothic romance, while the various elements that make up the three range over various themes. The two selves of the hero and heroine who are, in the logic of the romance, created only for being conjoined, are impossibly separated and distanced until the end of the narrative. "They walked in silence toward the river, side by side but eternally divided" (Beverley, 256). The keeping apart of the heroine and the hero creates a thirdness that comes between. This thirdness can be many things, but its liminal status gives it a ghostliness. Like a wraith, it wanders thinly in between two worlds of meaning. Out of place and unwanted, it points to the sadness of ruin, desecration, lost truths.

Yet we find that the origins of the erotic historical are even further troubled and complicated. Separate but related, existing alongside both the gothic and the erotic historical, the regency romance must be located in this history, as does its centerpiece: the dandy. The dandy hero manages to be as ruined as other dangerous lovers, but his blighted life focuses on superficialities such as fashion, sumptuousness, and empty dissipation. The regency romance (set during the English Regency—1811–1820) follows a strict formula: the wealthy aristocratic dandy's debauched lifestyle—his late-night drinking; his affairs with elegant but cruel women; his sophisticated dalliance with fine horses, clothes, balls, and gaming "hells"—points to the desolation of his life in the midst of the world of the cynical, empty *ton* and to his ultimate need of either transformation or dissolution.[19] The world of the regency romance is a very singular one; it even has its very own language, primarily developed from Georgette Heyer's influential regencies. The world Heyer conjures into being is based on actual historical dandified men of the Regency period (most famously, the ur-dandy Beau Brummell) and their literary depiction in the Silver-Fork novel (of the mid-nineteenth century).[20] In the regency romance (unlike the Silver-Fork novel) the modish and urbane rake must be reformed by an outsider—an unsophisticated, usually unfashionable girl, often an orphan and poor or working for a living. Her love electrifies his flagging interest in life and all its duties: through her he becomes a useful member of society.

The Duke of Avon in Heyer's *These Old Shades* (1926), like the Silver-Fork novel heroes Pelham (from Edward Bulwer-Lytton's novel of that name) and Trebeck (from Thomas Henry Lister's *Granby*), suffers from ennui as he strolls languidly about in jewels; a waistcoat of flowered silk; a long purple cloak, rose-lined.[21] Emotions "fatigue" him; passion brings a "sneer" to his face. Always cynical and sarcastic except in one arena—his "foppish appearance"—the Regency dandy is the exhausted self, living in the boredom of utter lassitude, of weariness. He expresses a serious interest only in rich clothing and such externals rather than an inner life, and he finds restless energy only when it comes to revenge on those men who slighted him in the past and blocked his intrigues with women. The duke, hardened and imperviously masked, has "no soul"—lost in his youth through ruthless treatment by others. His devilish depletion begins to shift and change when he "buys" a beautiful young boy out of forced labor at a sordid inn and makes him his page.[22] The boy worships the duke like a "slave" and what seems to be a homoerotic situation develops. However, the page is really the heroine in disguise, something the duke has guessed from the start. His Grace has taken in this girl/boy, Leonie, as part of his complicated revenge plot: he knows Leonie is the firstborn of the House of Saint-Vire, switched at birth with the son of farmers so the estates would not pass to a hated brother. Leonie amorously ensnares the duke and saves him from his self-hatred by the complicated mix of her dependence on him, her willfulness, and her crass volubility. The unfamiliarity of the heroine astonishes emotions out of the duke, such as care and sentiment, moving him into the romance's transcendental discourse of love. Leonie's outspokenness punctures the duke's urbane, cool sarcasm and his levity about a life meaningless to him. It is her very existence outside the codes of elegant society and her difficulty in reading these codes that causes a breakdown of his semiotic system. Replacing the stylish devil-may-care mask, the discourse of love fashions an interiority for the duke. Living at the limit with reckless carelessness, the dandy embodies two types of Byronism. The secretive misanthrope whose pained existence can be traced in plots of revenge against those who ruined his life comes from *The Giaour* and "The Corsair," and the life of idle love and cynical worldliness clearly echo *Don Juan*.[23]

The regency romance manages, interestingly enough, to mock the false Byronic pose at the same time it affirms the attraction of "real" Byronic heroes. Representations of the dangerous lover always play along this edge: at any moment they can cross the line into parody. In the regency, "true" Byronism lies in the man who, although failed and deeply wounded, can be redeemed by love. Thus truth lies at the heart of the fall—without the deeps of failure, one loses authenticity. In Heyer's *Venetia* (1958), Oswald, a superfluous boy, obsesses about Byronic darkness. Everyone sees through his attempts to be Byronic to attract Venetia: "The top of his desire is to be mistaken for the Corsair. He combs his hair into wild curls, knots silken handkerchiefs round his neck, and broods over the dark passions of his soul" (36). Venetia's aunt also plays at being Byronic along a different vein; she diets like Byron did, drinking vinegar, soda water, and then eating biscuits. Sublime insatiability has become merely a plan for dieting or a pose to attract women, both of which are unsuccessful.

Lord Dameral, the "Wicked Baron" whose reputation for orgies and liaisons with "sullied" women precedes him when he visits his country estates to escape his debts, at first appears dangerous and Byronic to Venetia, although she doesn't fear him and is hardly even impressed by this magnetism. "He bore himself with a faint suggestion of swashbuckling arrogance. As he advanced upon her Venetia perceived that he was dark, his countenance lean and rather swarthy, marked with lines of dissipation. A smile was curling his lips, but Venetia thought she had never seen eyes so cynically bored" (32). The shell of boredom must be pierced by the hardheaded, unshockable Venetia to reach the soft inside: the ardent, earnest young man encrusted by layers and layers of disillusionment. Instantaneously falling in love with Venetia, Dameral's subjectivity reaches a transfiguration.

In the regency romance much of the ability to see through society's transparent materialism resides in the heroine; she is generally outside fashionable society and does not desire to be in it. A domestic traditionalist, the regency heroine must convert the hero into seeing fashion and even society itself as worthless. His reformation comes in the elevation of the couple over social ambitions. The Silver-Fork novel dandy, on the contrary, when he is written into a didactic bildungsroman narrative, must finally step down from his rebellious pedestal of self and find his life's work among and for people, thus following a common mid-Victorian value.

II. Heideggerian Proximity

The dangerous lover narrative exemplifies, in its movements and its central concerns, the angst of being itself. The unfathomable mystery of existence in the world and the longing it perpetuates—the longing to fully *be*, to be sure what to do with the world that surrounds us—is the same desire the heroine of the romance has for the dangerous beloved. This is the desire to desire; it is desire per se. Such existential longing was Heidegger's lifework, and his ontological theories of proximity—or failed proximity—anatomize essential longing.[24] Heidegger's theory unravels the paradox of the way the hero and heroine move toward yet away from each other. The movement begins with an essential confusion: what would appear to be nearest, in its familiarity, homeliness, or *heimlichkeit,* and the most easily accessible and handy, lies furthest away from what is authentically most our own. Paradoxically then, what is truly nearest to one is what is most unfamiliar, strange, and *angst* producing. Moving closer authentically or with understanding causes what is familiar to withdraw. Christopher Fynsk characterizes this movement not as circular but rather "in terms of a paradoxical structure of simultaneous approach and withdrawal, of a casting forth that casts back" (41). It is what Heidegger calls the "everyday" that begins this ontological misunderstanding. Dasein's (Heidegger's word for our basic being) everyday way of being is entanglement in the average, which is an evasion and flight from the authentic possibilities of one's being. This is one of the fundamental structures of Dasein: the tendency to understand oneself through the immediate surrounding world nearest to one, an average "work-world" where useful objects are encountered. This world of "useful things" includes the "they"—the public that represents an averageness, "which prescribes what can and may be ventured, watches over every exception, which thrusts itself to the fore . . . [thus], every mystery loses its power." The "they" creates a "leveling down of all possibilities of being" (*Being and Time,* 127).[25] Because a constitutive factor of Dasein is to (mis)understand itself in regard to what appears to be nearest, in its average everyday working, it becomes entangled in the everyday, not understanding that there is a more authentic Dasein, which is actually nearer, covered over by this "tranquilized" being. Akin to the power of mystery, authentic being drops one out of an average everyday life into the purely individual, into a dwelling with the mystery of the unremitting aloneness of solitary being. Authentic Dasein comes from understanding oneself as one's own possibilities—as a singular, finite being—rather than as what is already real and available as a part of "publicness." In an authentic "kind of coming near," Heidegger writes, "one does not tend toward making something real available and taking care of it, but as one comes nearer understandingly, the possibility of the possible only becomes 'greater'"(*Being and Time,* 262).[26] For Dasein to come near in this way—which we could call a kind of transcendence—is to see all that is real, that could be "spelled out," withdraw.

Heidegger emphasizes, "The nearest nearness of being-toward-death as possibility is as far removed as possible from anything real" (*Being and Time,* 262).[27] The situation of this nearness to greater and greater possibility, or to a kind of unknown, lies somehow "inside" one—as possibilities that belong only to this individual Dasein. With this nearness, one draws closer and closer to what is both the most obscure and the most free—a freeing of all possibility—yet still what is so close that it is one's own existence itself. Blanchot describes this type of nearness as a proximity that retains its unknownness because one does not have the distance to see it, just as each individual, living away in the busyness and hurry of a life, will not be able to trace out the larger truth of that life. He explains closeness itself as " . . . an experience that one will represent to oneself as being strange and even as the experience of strangeness. But if it is so, let us recognize that it is this not because it is too removed. On the contrary, it is so close that we are prohibited from taking any distance from it—it is foreign in its very proximity" (*Infinite,* 45).

The progress of the dangerous lover romance follows the misdirectedness, the willful error, which is part of being in the world. While in the end union and closure occur, along the way flight from the beloved and the evasion of union describe the basic plot structure of most romances (and this is especially true for the erotic historical). Immanent love can only come at the very end: the complete presence of both lovers, as equally confessed lovers, beloved together in the same place and at the same time. All meaning is then finally immanent and this is the final aim, or the climax and ending of the book. This full presence of love is the love story's meaning; everything in the narrative means this, and this is all it means. Love's completion defines romance; love's presence constitutes the end of the story and all events tend toward this culmination. Yet "to tend toward" here means to flee, to cover over, and, at the same time, to always be in a movement toward. Here is the strange movement of ontology itself—the moving closer which causes familiar nearness to withdraw. The structure of this proposition—the fleeing movement of love—lies in withheld secrets, postponements, misunderstandings, and evasion.[28] Jean-Luc Nancy sees love as an "infinity of shatters." "There is no master figure, there is no major representation of love, nor is there any common assumption of its scattered and inextricable shatters . . . love itself misses . . . it comes *across* and never simply *comes* to its place or to term" (*Inoperative Community,* 102).

Ontologically, we flee authentic being and become entangled in the everyday. Flight and entanglement in the dangerous lover romance occur through the almost ubiquitous plot device of the undisclosed secret(s) between the hero and heroine, providing numerous postponements of the climax. Both the hero and the heroine keep secrets from each other, causing misunderstandings and distance. In Barbara Dawson Smith's *Seduced by a Scoundrel,*[29] the heroine, Alicia Pemberton, is deliberately deceived by the hero, Drake Wilder, into thinking that he is a heartless gambler who wants only to antagonize her. He does this because he plots to hide the truth of his paternity, until the right moment, which will maximize his revenge on his father who has refused to acknowledge him as his son. This secret pain, this strange and unfamiliar interiority, causes Alicia to flee him as someone who frightens her and will betray her love. Yet she is, finally, evading her beloved, her final ending. It is fated that what she flees—the terror of the unknown other—is what will finally engulf her, when secrets are exteriorized in amorous unity. In Dorothy Garlock's *Wind of Promise*,[30] the hero, Kain Debolt, must be cold and distant toward the heroine, Vanessa, even though he has fallen deeply in love with her because he thinks he is dying of stomach cancer. He cannot disclose this information to her because he does not want her to see him as sick and vulnerable, and thus less of a man. He must constantly push her away; she becomes confused and thinks he is her enemy. Yet the erotic charge is located just here: in this secret she senses.

> Kain said the words simply, and Vanessa turned to look at him. She was surprised to see a deep sadness in his golden brown eyes, and a flood of tenderness and longing swept through her body.
>
> On seeing that smile, Kain felt the full pain of his regret. (99–100)

Secret sadness causes longing to sweep through her body because this sadness contains the unknowability of the other. Derrida uses the idea of the secret to describe the utterly singular, the other as other. The secret is that which "we speak of but are unable to say"; it is "the sharing of what is not shared" (*A Taste for the Secret*, 58). In approaching the beloved, the secret of his singular being is witnessed but is never fully disclosed; the secret becomes the sadness of closeness to the beloved other. In writing of jealousy, Peggy Kamuf describes the impossible desire of the lover to know the other in his singularity. The beloved, and any possible knowledge of him, is subject to the boundaries of the phenomenality of the object, he "appears; appearing, he or she may also disappear or dissimulate" (64). The failure to know the beloved fully, completely and without remainder, describes the erotic withdrawal, the distance from belonging of the dangerous lover romance.

Heidegger sees truth, or *aletheia,* as an act of uncovering, or the unhidden. The desire of both philosophy and romance is to reveal the truth, to illuminate it and bring it to a confession. The loved one envelops and imprisons unknown worlds, which must be deciphered.[31] The erotically charged removal of the veil points to the spark from which this erotic originates—the veil itself. The hiding and the disclosing of the secret both create eroticism. From *Seduced:* "She wanted to feel the warmth of Drake's arms around her. She wanted to learn all of the secrets of his past . . ." (Smith, 206). It is in the very flight *from* the beloved, through postponement by the secret that the strongest erotic tensions shake the ground of being. Postponement *is* the erotic. Hence the evasion of imminent love—thematically the transcendence or sublime in romance—enacts paradoxically a moving closer to an everyday familiarity, away from a secretive estrangement in flight and evasion. Yet evasion is also always already a move toward the full presence of meaning—the full confessions of all secrets at the climax of the book.

The heroine has other ways of "withdrawing" from the dangerous lover. When the heroine draws near to the hero through everyday means such as sight, touch, and discourse, the immanence of love appears to fail because this nearness is misread as something other than love. Misunderstandings abound in the romance genre: he pulls away from kissing her because, out of love for her, he doesn't want his blightedness to hurt her; she thinks he doesn't desire her. What will finally be love is sidetracked into other valences such as loss of self-worth and will; or the equation of sex with love, required for this plot, will go awry, becoming domesticated and miniaturized as a "one-night stand," "pure lust," or "open hostility." Fynsk discusses how Dasein, as essentially structured, misinterprets. Most clearly seen through Dasein's relation to language, the double movement of nearness creates a kind of danger. Language is "the most dangerous" because through it "man stands exposed in the 'proximity and distance of the essence of things'" (189).[32] Like Dasein, another register of the evasion of the beloved is misreading, generally of the eyes and the face. The heroine and sometimes the hero of this formula are bad readers. Often misreading occurs through not knowing the language, the gestures of the other, which are fugitive and migrant to such an extent that they cannot be deciphered. Eyes are points of mystery; they speak of the possibility of transcendence in romance, and hence they are often misread. Things that flash in character's eyes contain lost scenes of access and end up closing off possibility, at least for a hundred or so pages, rather than opening it. In Smith's novel, Alicia attempts to read Drake's eyes. "Something flashed in his eyes, a starkness she couldn't read" (178).

> "I wonder," she mused, "if you *want* me to think badly of you." For
> a heartbeat, something flashed in his eyes. Something that came
> and went so quickly, she couldn't be sure if it was surprise or annoy-
> ance. Or something else entirely. (164)

Because the other can never be known, Alicia misinterprets, seeing this flash as anger, hostility, or something undefined which points to his scoundrelhood. Unlike the romantic truism that the eyes are mirrors to the soul, here the eyes show the soul only through a darkened, cloudy glass. Or, eyes here are true mirrors, reflecting only the one looking, in all her unsureness and ontological instability, rather than being a clear river to the truth of the soul. In *Lord of Danger*[33] the heroine thinks, "As usual, his expression was impossible to read" (226). In *Lord of Midnight*,[34] Claire describes Renald as a "cryptic script" (234). "What was he thinking? She had no idea. She longed for a spontaneous word or gesture by which to judge him, but he was as incomprehensible as a text she'd once seen written in the Arabic script" (65). He envelops a secret space the heroine would like to plumb. The hardness of his exterior, like a mask, presents a cryptogram or a blank page. The heroine will eventually crack the code, which is only the discovery of one word—love. The phrase "I love you" presents the completion of the narrative. In the discourse of love, Barthes writes, language's meaning becomes suspended, and the sentence points only to pure affect. "Amorous *dis-cursus* is not dialectical; it turns like a perpetual calendar, an encyclopedia of affective culture" (*Lover's Discourse,* 7). The words of the lover are pure singular presence, and hence the "I love you" must be repeated again and again in order to attempt to recreate the original avowal.

Another scene of misunderstanding in the romance involves hearing. Often the hero mutters things under his breath. The heroine doesn't understand these murmurings, although clearly they are presages of the final end. "Through the heat haze of her own passion, she heard Luke mutter something beneath his breath and then he was kissing her mouth . . ." (Jordan, 161).[35] "And she could hear it [intense desire] in the harsh sound of the air escaping from his lungs as he muttered something unintelligible under his breath and then, leaning back against the wall, urged her between his parted thighs" (Jordan, 142). To hear the beloved is to fail to comprehend the whispers and garbled words that mean nothing other than love, repeated in an enchanted speech, suspended of meaning other than that the secret will be disclosed.

Fraught with fiery pits and sudden chasms, the way to love in the romance symbolizes the radical difference of the other. In the movement to summon the infinite, the lovers run up against finitude again and again.[36] These series of failures point to an important difference between romance and pornography. Pornography is always a utopia, hence Steven Marcus's term "pornotopia." In pornography, everyone reaches immediate success and final fulfillment because men always have erections at the right moment; women always desire what the man wants to give them; the orgasm happens right on time, simultaneously, for both parties. In pornography, everything comes into sexual usage, all objects and subjects are part of the sexual play. A tree in a pornographic scene becomes erotic because it is a secret place to have sex. A telephone's only use is to set up a sexual rendezvous. Conversation's meaning lies only in its device as seduction. In the dystopic world of romance, everything acts as a catalyst to pull the hero and heroine apart: all senses, discourse, and objects are sites and scenes of failure. Here we are in amorous time, where impulse and act do not coincide, where speaking and understanding miss their proper destination.

Unlike pornography, then, in the dangerous lover romance failure also comes with the evasion or covering over of love through misunderstanding seduction, or ravishment. The missed arrival of love occurs through a doubled misreading, both of the heroine herself and the hero. In the romance, sex between the hero and heroine is never solely a material or physical act; hence it doesn't contain the "meatiness" or purely transparent usage of sex in pornography, which is merely to "get off." Sex in the romance always must lead to an excess of meaning, the full presence of love. Because it is a possible point of access to transcendence, like the eyes and their flashing, sex constructs a site of Heideggerian nearness; sex creates a continued failure of presence. The heroine misreads her own sexual desire as, rather than the presence of love, "merely" a lack of contained control on her part, or an embarrassing weakness of the senses, or a too-passionate sensuality which she must avoid; otherwise she might be seduced into a loveless affair. She doesn't understand that she is always already in love with him—dazzlement at first sight, so to speak, or on the first page. In Rosemary Rogers's *A Dangerous Man*,[37] many of these false arrivals occur, with an initial ravishment and then later regrets.

> Her mouth opened to . . . protest? surrender? . . . and his tongue slid inside in a sizzling exploration that shocked a moan from her. . . . Her head fell back, and all thought of resistance faded into something else, strange new emotions he had somehow awakened in her, emotions that made her cling to him. . . . (82)

> But inside, she was sick with the knowledge that she had once more ignored convention and wisdom and decency to throw herself at a man who took her casually and then discarded her just as casually. But what had she thought? That he would declare himself in love with her? That he would beg her to go away with him? No, that sort of thing happened only in romantic tales, not in real life. (183)

What is covered over here is the authentic meaning of this event—the touch and feel of the radiance of the beloved's body—and meaning is evaded through an everyday publicness of sex equaling lust, a one-night stand, or open hostility, rape. Hence the structure of a paradoxical move toward while moving away occurs, where the most intimate erotic, or what feels to be the closest, the most familiar touch, pulls the hero and heroine away from each other into an increasingly solitary, melancholy despair. The despair—she wants him but she will only have him if he really loves her, which she is convinced that he does not, generally because of his "dangerousness," his secretiveness, misanthropy, etc.—will finally lead to full meaning itself. Another example of this erotic near/far is Haywood Smith's *Border Lord*.[38]

> Slowly, deliberately, Duncan approached her, blatant hunger in his eyes.
>
> What did he mean to do? Catherine's arms tightened around Nevin, her heart beating faster. Part of her wanted to flee, but the greater part of her wanted Duncan Maxwell to kiss her again. (192)

Misinterpreting the touch of the hero opens chasms of confusion. The question above, "What did he mean to do?" is a mainstay in this formula, clearly dating back to the Gothic heroine confronted by the villain where the question legitimately takes on a serious coloring: "Does he mean to kill me? Rape me? Lock me up in a dungeon?" Generally, in the contemporary dangerous lover romance, the heroine believes the hero does not love her but merely desires her sexually or even hates her and wants revenge through seduction or rape. She lives "tranquilized" in the everydayness of "everyone feels lust, hence that is what he (and I) feels" and thus evades the end and finite destiny, her final meaning that leads to thematic transcendence. At the same time, the erotic can be located just here: in the evasion, in the failure, and in the covering over of presence. In each of these plot tensions can be found both the failure and a movement of or toward success; each moment compresses contradictions into a seed ready for germination.

Rife with paradoxes, the dangerous lover stands, in a Modernist sense, always in between. The one who fails yet holds the most power; who describes with his subjectivity the infinite yet can be read through and through by a glance at his face; who is never so close to his beloved as when he appears irreparably severed from her; who arrives at the end of the romance united and whole, yet is the one always falling apart. Romance as a genre, although defined by its wholeness—by the progress of two people coming closer to oneness or being pulled apart from the oneness that seems inevitable, but finally coming to an end in a union, a whole narrative—centers on a character whose subjectivity does not hold together. His narrative runs up against discontinuity, where pieces of his present come from a past that seems utterly lost. His self fragments along lines of pained forgottenness, along hateful openings into nothingness. As beloved, pieces of him are picked up by the other, an attempt is made to fit them together, to pull together a concept of self, an entity with enough substance to be loved, to place hope in. In some sense the space between fragments holds the love, is the residence of love's movement. The parts of the subject that gap open, that make the self, in some radical way, not a self, hold the possibility of loving the dangerous lover in a kind of stasis of two opposing possibilities: love and the impossibility of loving nothingness. Love becomes creative, based on reconstituting the beloved again and again. Benjamin elaborates a theory of hidden love, wherein love's secrecy comes through loving the parts of the other that no one else could love:

> If the theory is correct that feeling is not located in the head, that we sentiently experience a window, a cloud, a tree not in our brains but rather in the place where we see it, then we are, in looking at our beloved, too, outside ourselves. But in a torment of tension and ravishment. Our feeling, dazzled, flutters like a flock of birds in the women's radiance. And as birds seek refuge in the leafy recesses of a tree, feelings escape into the shaded wrinkles, the awkward movements and inconspicuous blemishes of the body we love, where they can lie low in safety. And no passerby would guess that it is just here, in what is defected and censurable, that the fleeting darts of adoration nestle. (*Selected Writings,* 1:449)

Benjamin explains how the beloved's body fragments in shadowy pieces, like the dead body that decays, becoming something altogether different than it was before. Haloed with a shadowy nimbus of desire, mystery, and an impossible insubstantialness, the specterlike other moves and haunts.

CHAPTER TWO

The Spectral Other and Erotic Melancholy

The Gothic Demon Lover and the Early Seduction Narrative Rake (1532–1822)

There was a laughing Devil in his sneer,
That raised emotions both of rage and fear;
And where his frown of hatred darkly fell,
Hope withering fled—and Mercy sighed farewell!
—Byron

I. The Gothic Villain

We remember the fascination of the villain from when we were children: Captain Hook, the old hag in "Hansel and Gretel," the Wicked Witch of the West. As T. S. Eliot recognized, "It is better, in a paradoxical way, to do evil than to do nothing: at least, we exist" (344). The Romantics, those poets who always admired the view from the eyes of the child, were everywhere mesmerized by the villain, by strangeness in beauty, by the corrupt, the contaminated, the imperiled.[1] The Brontës held onto the richness of their childhood imaginations and from this kept treasure Rochester and Heathcliff emerge. Yet Rochester was not the first character to wrap up the contradictions of lover and enemy into one subjectivity. The tragic hero whose main energy comes from villainous actions, self-destructive impulses, or character flaws can be traced back to Elizabethan and Jacobean tragedy, and even earlier, to the Nietzschean will-to-power of Machiavelli's *The Prince* (1532). Such early magnetic scoundrels range from the cursed ambitions of the ur-seeker-of-other-worldly-knowledge, Marlowe's *Faustus* (c. 1588); Promus, the just man who wrestles with his desire for Cassandra and loses in George Whetstone's *Promus and Cassandra* (1578); and Guise in Fulke Greville's *Alaham* (1590s), who displays the sublime but wasted

29

subjectivity of the Byronic hero. An erotics of evil develops out of these characters and their ambitious will for destruction coupled with the genius of an all-seeing eye. Shakespeare's *Richard III* (1592–94) combines a dreaded cruelty with a witty intellect and an insatiable drive.[2] *Hamlet* (1600–1601) brings into this history the important characteristic of the tragedy of impotent melancholy, a sense of a world too barren for action, for an attempt at change.

Running through Jacobean tragedy, the tormented, sympathetic reprobate appears in such characters as Vindice in Cyril Tourneur's *The Revenger's Tragedy* (1607); the atheist, D'Amville, in *The Atheist's Tragedy* (1611); and Giovanni in John Ford's *'Tis a Pity She's a Whore* (1633). Lucifer in Milton's *Paradise Lost* (1667), the serpentine tempter of Eve, falls from grace as later dangerous lovers will. And Eve's seduction by this demon lover, causing her own fall from grace, is repeated again and again in the erotic historical where the heroine, after her seduction by the devilish rogue, becomes outcast with him. As Gilbert and Gubar point out, this gives a new meaning to the "fall" in "to fall in love." And this fall stands always in relation to knowledge, whether it be occult knowledge, which gives one too much power to live in the world, or a cynical knowledge that comes to know the world too well, emptying it of mystery and possibility. Luciferian dangerous lovers always cut a devilish figure with their sneering rebellion and refusal to bow to any power but that of their own tortured subjectivity.

Considered by many to be the first romance (some even call it the first novel), Samuel Richardson's *Pamela, or Virtue Rewarded* (1740–41) places the villain as both the heroine's worst foe and her final blessing for virtuous behavior. An early example of the reformed rake formula, *Pamela* centers around the scoundrel/suitor Mr. B., who plots Pamela's ruin by seducing her but, so impressed is he by her strict sense of the virtuous and dutiful place of a young serving maid, he marries her instead.[3] In *Pamela,* as well as in the Gothic, eroticism resides in texts—letters that Pamela keeps in her "bosom" and then are purloined by Mr. B. While these missives masquerade as virtuous tracts on how to stay away from a scheming rake, they become a nexus for erotic activity with Pamela's flurried excitement in her letter writing, her exhaustive recording of the minutiae of her seduction, and her bringing the texts to bed—nailing Mr. B's sadistic letter to her bedstead as a masochistic reminder to "be good." The letter even becomes a substitute for sex when Mr. B. reads Pamela's letters instead of continuing his seduction. The highest point of sexual satiation *is* the text, and furthermore, the text that does not reach its proper destination (her letters are addressed to her parents).[4] These dead letters represent the love that becomes, at least temporarily, a kind of dead letter: love is misunderstanding itself.[5]

In Radcliffe, the most romantic of the Gothic novelists, the virtuous heroes are quickly forgotten; in their paleness they fall away next to the bold chiaroscuro shine of the cruel villain.[6] The villains in much of the Gothic create the central development and complexity of the narrative by their inexplicably meaningful actions, their deeply perturbed spirits which precipitously race toward ruin on a grand scale. These villains and their violent machinations against the heroine's virtue steal the show while the characterless lover is lost in the background with his transparent tenderness and adoration.[7] Both Schedoni in Radcliffe's *The Italian* and Ambrosio in Matthew Lewis's *The Monk* contain the erotic complexities and fascination of a manifold and fearful enemy, while the lover in contrast seems easily read. Schedoni's fallen greatness and gloomy violence disclose a hidden world of darkness and death.

> There were circumstances, however, which appeared to indicate him to be a man of birth, and of fallen fortune; his spirit . . . seemed lofty; it shewed not, however, the aspirings of a generous mind, but rather the gloomy pride of a disappointed one. . . . Some few persons in the convent . . . believed that the peculiarities of his manners . . . were the effect of misfortunes preying upon a haughty and disordered spirit, while others conjectured them the consequence of some hideous crime gnawing upon an awakened conscience. . . . His figure was striking . . . there was something terrible in its air; something almost superhuman . . . gave an effect to his large melancholy eye, which approached to horror . . . and his eyes were so piercing that they seemed to penetrate, at a single glance, into the hearts of men, and to read their most secret thoughts. . . . (34–35)

His penetrating glance exposes the hidden body of the other, without itself showing anything, making the other's interiority known. Schedoni's melancholy self magnetically pulls the other who desires to know; he is like an emptiness which draws in a material to fill it. In *The Monk,* a Gothic bildungsroman, Ambrosio begins as the adored "Man of Holiness" but develops into a corrupted malefactor when he is seduced by a temptress disguised as a monk (herself a dangerous lover).

The Gothic enemy moves, changes, hides a riveting past and future, while the Gothic lover's insipidity comes from his stasis as a character, his ability to be only one thing. The Brontës knew this in spades. With the collapse of the blackguard and sweetheart into one Rochester, Brontë can begin her story with the intriguing Gothic stranger, and only later transform him into the domesticated and dependent lover. The evil double contained in a single character is itself a Gothic mainstay, as in James Hogg's

Confessions of a Justified Sinner (an interesting case of a homoerotic haunting by a devil-self). A variation on this theme is being haunted by a double represented in another subjectivity, as in Mary Shelley's *Frankenstein*
and William Godwin's *Caleb Williams.* In post–Gothic Victorian novels,
these Gothic doubles continue to proliferate, as in *The Strange Case of Dr.
Jekyll and Mr. Hyde, The Picture of Dorian Gray,* and even *Jane Eyre* with
Bertha as Jane's double.

II. The Erotic Uncanny

To love the dangerous lover is to feel the creepy uncanniness of finding the
familiar at the heart of terrifying strangeness. It is to love the uneasiness,
the restless uncertainty, the inquietude of never fully knowing: when we'll
die, if we'll find true love. A theory of the eroticism of the uncanny can be
developed from the dangerous lover narrative; such a theory begins with
the Gothic proper of the late eighteenth century and then moves through
the nineteenth century to the contemporary Gothic-themed romance.
Heidegger, like Freud, interests himself in the etymology of this word—
unheimlich. Both point to the "*heim,*" or "home" at the heart, but
Heidegger is primarily interested in its meaning of "unhomeliness" as in
"not-at-home." Heidegger sees the being "not-at-home" as a kind of
angst—as eliciting the terror and anxiety of existential unease. Dasein feels
"at home" when it loses itself in the ease and happy familiarity of what's
close at hand. When Dasein turns away from easy everydayness, toward
the essential truth of being, it feels uncanny because it is "not-at-home";
it stands utterly singular and alone in the world, "individualized to itself,"
and "absolutely unmistakable to itself" (*Being and Time,* 256). In fact
"uncanniness is the fundamental kind of being-in-the-world" (*Being and
Time,* 277). Hence, when Dasein draws closest to itself, it is nearest to its
most mysterious and uncertain possibility. But we can take this even further: when Dasein understands its absorption in the "they" as an evasion
and tranquilization and turns away from it into essential being, then not
only does Dasein feel a sense of being "not-at-home" in its essence, but the
comfortable "home" of everydayness also no longer belongs to one. The
potential for uncanniness then permeates the movement (which is itself
always possible) of Dasein within both the everyday and essential being.
Face-to-face with its own being, Dasein's uncanny feeling is not just a
sense of being "not-at-home," it is also a sense of this strangeness being
itself at the heart of one's own existence. Uncanniness has a close kinship
to the theory of proximity explored in chapter 1—the strange push/pull
of attraction to the dangerous lover. The uncanny also uncovers the mis-

understanding at the heart of being: the way we think the most familiar—the everyday world around us, full of people, society, and chatter—constitutes our true being. But our authentic self is only to be found on the edge of the abyss, at the limit of darkness, of the dizzy rapture of the unknowable. Meeting the dangerous lover for the first time, the heroine discovers what will be, in the logic of the romance, her true self, her essential being, but which she initially regards as a deeply threatening other.

To survey Freud's ideas on the *unheimlich* in this context gives them a romantic coloring. Freud takes his idea of the uncanny further with his insight that concealment is an aspect of the work of the uncanny. Heidegger sees the uncanny merely as being "not-at-home"; he does not see concealment as integral to creating the uncanny. Freud describes an uncanny feeling—a "dread and creeping horror"—coming from, among other things, the revivification through an event or experience of an idea repressed or concealed in the hinter regions of the unconscious. "The 'uncanny' is that class of the terrifying which leads back to something long known to us, once very familiar" (369–70). Hence the uncanny brings about a "creepiness" not only because one feels "not-at-home" in the unfamiliar and strange experience, but also because, at the heart of the strange, there is a sense of home, of a deep interiority, of a place already visited. The already concealed, which is now partially or entirely disclosed, causes the uncanny to surface as a feeling. The full dreadfulness of this feeling comes from the fact that what is disturbing is located "inside" us, it "belongs" to us, individually, and we have been responsible for both producing and concealing it. Shelley's Victor Frankenstein has this reaction upon knowing his creation: Oh God, it's mine.

Another etymological thread related to "*heim*" is "*geheim*," which also has the "home" in it but means "secret" or "concealed." As explored in chapter 1, the "secret home" can be linked to the Heideggerian idea that, in an everyday way, authentic homes are "secret." This helps to unravel why the secret is such an important theme to the dangerous lover romance. The romantic heroine's potential, her "authentic" self, lies in the presence of love, in unconcealed, disclosed meaning. Her possibility as fully present to love is the secret behind all other secrets and this is her final "home"—her destiny, fate. "A cry sounded in her throat; then her legs parted and he was inside her. This was his true coming home, the only one that mattered" (Rogers, 287). And another "home" scene: " . . . that bewildering notion that somehow she had found that special wondrous place; that special wondrous person who was her real home, that knowledge somehow or other Luke had reached out and touched the very core of her innermost being and because of that . . . because of him the whole of her life would be changed forever" (Jordan, 155). And again:

"With that simple profession [of love], all the broken pieces of Catherine's life shaped themselves into a picture of perfect provision. Suddenly she saw how everything had worked to bring them to this wondrous moment" (Smith, 369). The hero also finds his home in the beloved. One hero thinks to himself, "he . . . had known the moment he looked at her that he was confronting his own fate" (Jordan, 424). For the heroine to draw closer to her essential self she must move nearer to an unsettling other who is her "home." Like Dasein, what has been concealed, the presence of the true love, is something that has been "known" all along. Hence the revelation of this love leads to the uncanny: "A heightened sensation of portent, of standing on the edge of something vital and life changing shook her, a feeling of uncannily clear-minded perception that suddenly, here and now . . . she was facing something immensely important" (Jordan, 316). And the uncanny moment reveals what was already there. "There was a wonderful, exhilarating sense of release and freedom . . . in being able to cast aside her guard and acknowledge, admit, that the desire for him, which she was now allowing to express itself, had been there virtually from the first time they met. It existed even if she herself had tried to force it underground and keep it hidden away" (Jordan, 328). The structure of this uncanny situates a sense of strangeness in the heart of what is one's own—the true love and final destiny in an other whose enemy-like surface at first repels. But, in that it discloses, the heroine also feels that it is something that has been "there" all along but that she has concealed. Instead of horror in the uncanny moment, in romance it is the titillating ache of the "Oh God, it's mine." So, in a sense, while it sometimes appears that the heroine is moving inexorably toward her fate, a mere puppet in the hands of the machinations of the hero, she is always in what is her "own"; her adventures emanate out from the dark center of her singular being. The hero can even be located inside her, like a ghost in the unconscious, or a closed box waiting to be broached: "She felt as though he had found a secret entrance into her belly, into her bones. She felt that he was folded inside her" (Doyle, 121).

With the romantic uncanny the moment opens up in all its complexity: each moment contains an uncovering of what one already knows and then a reconcealment of knowledge. The heroine already knows she is in love with the hero and she can see the movement of her narrative ending while at the same time she flees and evades this destiny. Thus the dangerous lover romance is filled with hesitancy, false starts, and frozen impotence. A dark madness of failure often overtakes these narratives, a sense of movement's terrifying inconceivability. The Gothic proper never fully resolves this madness. Even in Radcliffe, the happy ending feels like an anticlimatic, pasted-on addition—not very relevant to the terrors of the earlier story. But the gothic romance and the erotic historical interrupt this impotence with the final presence of the scene of union: "His mouth closed hungrily over hers in a moist, deep, endless kiss. It seemed to Vanessa that they were no longer two separate people, but one blended together by magic" (Garlock, 358). The reintegration of the strange self leads to an odd looping of time that both the reader and the heroine experience. The loop occurs because the end—union in love—is prefigured in the beginning, and all along, as it is at the same time concealed. So the end seems to be both a completion, a closure, and a return to an origin, to the beginning. The end doesn't feel like a narrative progression forward or a move backward, but the meeting of both the arrival and the setting off.

The heroine of the dangerous lover romance is like a haunted house: bumping about inside her is this other self—this enigmatic demon lover, full of secret gestures of longings. Yet the hauntedness of these narratives does not only happen on the level of the characters of the story; in fact, all narrativity contains a spectral element—characters come to life, are animated out of the darkness of nonexistence, point to an irreversible past, and then die again at the close of the narrative.[8] Narrative power moves in the shadowy realm of the revenant, the dead but still lifelike and illuminated, the remainder of the real. Making explicit the ghostliness of all narrative, the Gothic novel tells the story of those things that partake of or fall into relation to death—silence, secrets, imprisonment, and remorse. We are already aware of the importance of the secret to the dangerous lover narrative: love itself and its relation to a past, a history, creates a constellation of secret communications. Silences maintained on the most important matters, hidden facts that would save the lives of many, unfold the plot of Gothic novels as well as dark romances. The hero of both genres holds his subjectivity in secret. Maturin's *Melmoth the Wanderer* (1820) revolves around an impenetrable secret which is so unspeakable it throws the speaker who tries to utter it into fits or even causes death. The theme of wholesale tragedy springs readily from the impossibility of communicating one's inner meaning: "The very thirst of my body seemed to vanish in this fiery thirst of the soul for communication, where all communication was unutterable, impossible, hopeless. . . . The secret of silence is the only secret" (Maturin, 151). The blocked speech of the Gothic novel continues in the dangerous lover narrative: lovers who cannot speak their "inner meaning"—their love for the other—hold their essence in abeyance until the final transcendence of the narrative.

Melmoth, the Cain-like "disinherited child of nature" (245), sells his soul to the devil who curses him to wander the world forever, trying to ruin others' souls. Like later dangerous lovers, he becomes "the demon of superhuman misanthropy" (233). His "boundless aspiration after forbidden knowledge" (380) leads to the Faustian bargain that seals his fall from grace: "I hate all things that live—all things that are dead—I am myself hated and hateful" (244). Yet out of the ceaseless torment of a ruined life comes the glimmer of hope: atonement by a true love. He meets the innocent and beautiful Isadora, secretly visits her at night, and finally convinces her to participate in a clandestine marriage. Inexplicably failing at the crucial moment here and in a second incident with another "pure" woman, Melmoth just misses the discovery of "the ineffable and forbidden secret of his destiny" (238). His destiny, as the reader knows although she is never told, lies in the possibility of grace through the beloved. His only absolution lies in love, but this can never be. The Faustian bargain of the Gothic villain must always include the heroine as well—and this is one good reason for the impossibility of love with the Gothic villain. She must be doomed like him, in order to love him: love as the curse of Cain. Melmoth gnashes out, "'Seek all that is terrible in nature for your companions and your lover!—woo them to burn and blast you—perish in their fierce embrace, and you will be happier, far happier, than if you lived in mine! Lived!—Oh, who can be mine and live! . . . If you will be mine, it must be amid a scene like this for ever— amid fire and darkness—amid hatred and despair—amid—' and his voice swelling to a demoniac shriek of rage and horror, and his arms extended, as if to grapple with the fearful objects of some imaginary struggle . . ." (Maturin, 247). The frozen, impotent fury of the dangerous lover will be melted in later love narratives; the Gothic gives only an approach to the interruption, never the actual breaking through.

The obscure flash of meaning, the secret affinity, important both to the Gothic and the dangerous lover romance, draw the lover to her beloved. We can liken this fragmented, obscured meaning and the disjointed piecing together of narrative to Benjamin's envisioning of historicity, or ur-history (*Urgeschichte*). He sees historicity not as a series of statements about major events and famous people but rather as a collection of secret affinities discoverable only by indirect means and chance occurrences. Meaning comes not through the creation of continuity, teleology, and connective narrativity, but rather through the side-by-sideness of fragments, the flash of the image.[9] The dangerous lover's subjectivity, his narrativity, or history, similarly shatters into a handful of unexplained pieces like the curiosities in the cabinet of the collector. To communicate with this bundle of meanings, the lover of the dangerous beloved must discover secret affinities, dreamlike understandings that are never fully explained. Thus might she create an obscure dialogue, an amatory conversation. This dialogue, like Benjamin's history, occurs in flashes, maintaining an obscure stasis, a dark certainty. Knowledge manifests itself in hiddenness here; knowledge does not occur in the realm of enlightenment. And this knowledge, which also obscures knowledge, is a kind of sight or an insight (a sight inside) that brings an understanding of subterranean affinities. The singularity of the hero and heroine's love and the reasons for their coming together are something only they can know. The simple characterization and plots of many important dangerous lover romances express the sense that there need be no drawn-out explanation for love; in fact, it can never be explained. This silent meaning describes the absolute singularity of love and points to its seeming fatefulness, its unexplainable, unhistorical presentness. Here it is; it appears out of darkness, carrying with it always this darkness. Silence keeps the lovers both joined and standing in a nomadic tandem to the rest of the social order, always on the outside of what they are near. Their secret joining happens in a darkness that blinds, subsumes. Whispering, mumbled communications, as stated in the last chapter, are the ways the dangerous lover inscribes meaning. Like the effaced manuscripts in *Melmoth the Wanderer,* where the essence of the story has decayed, been ripped off, or smudged, the dangerous lover's meaning never quite arrives.

III. Love as Mourning

Because of their beginnings in the Gothic proper, the erotic historical and the gothic romance are rooted in a relation to death, to loss, to pining. The dangerous lover often takes the figure of the mourner; for him, consciousness itself can become mourning, the lamenting of a bitter present and the obsession with lost bliss. Sad wastedness and a pale longing become erotic.[10] His self is defined by what he doesn't have, and his melancholy guarantees the constant reopening of his desires.[11] The heavy, hanging head, the dark furrowed brow express a disconsolate interiority, a constant longing for already-lost love. As Proust remarks, the only real paradise is the one we have lost.

In the interstice of the Gothic and the erotic historical lies the seminal romance on death's linkage with love—*Wuthering Heights*. If we say that *Wuthering Heights* tells the story of a particular kind of love—one full of passionate mourning—then the very narrative structure takes on the black garb of this love.[12] Because the story starts after Catherine has already died, their love narrative begins doomed. The whole story moves forward toward this inexorable end which has already occurred. The dying of the other and the possibility of love's death suffuse the book, but it is not the silence of death that resounds, but the noisiness of the struggle against preordained fate, as befits a dangerous lover. In the first scene between the lovers—a

bedroom one—the dead Catherine ~~haunts~~ the living Heathcliff, and the
dreams of the dead bring on all the wretched pains of living when the
beloved other is unreachable. When Heathcliff hears of Lockwood's dream
of the child-Catherine trying to come in out of the cold, he expresses his
violent longing to cross into that place where Catherine is, to bridge the
gap between the living and the dead. "He got up on to the bed, and
wrenched open the lattice, bursting, as he pulled at it, into an uncontrollable passion of tears. 'Come in! Come in!' he sobbed. 'Cathy, do come.
Oh, do—*once* more! Oh! My heart's darling! Hear me *this* time, Catherine,
at last!'" (27). Catherine has, in a sense, always been dead. The child-ghost
who visits Lockwood's dreams in the beginning of the book states that she
has "been a waif for twenty years" (21). This would mean she dies as a
child, when she is still together with Heathcliff, running wild on the
moors. This haunting waif embodies their love as always existing on the
outside—of living, of substantiality, of time and place. Their love dies yet
always persists. After her death, Catherine's self seems to flit, shadowlike,
all around Heathcliff. "I cannot look down to this floor, but her features
are shaped on the flags! In every cloud, in every tree—filling the air at
night, and caught by glimpses in every object, by day I am surrounded
with her image!" (278). Not only is Heathcliff's very life force, Catherine,
as insubstantial as the merest breeze but she also resides within him, as
Steve Vine asserts: "Heathcliff encrypts a lost life" (138). Vine utilizes
Abraham and Torok's theories on encryptment—the entombing of a lost
other within the subject when that subject refuses to mourn, or let go, of
the dead other. In his refusal to mourn, Heathcliff becomes Catherine's
tomb. Catherine takes on a whole life within this tomb—a life which
attempts to draw Heathcliff inside himself, which would mean death for
him. The uncanny core of Heathcliff's subjectivity is Catherine as the
object just out of reach. But Catherine also encrypts Heathcliff when she
finds the actual, living Heathcliff tormenting and unfamiliar. She wants
the child-Heathcliff back, the one who was hers—her own love. Close to
her death, during a fit of anger at him, she says in his presence: "That is
not *my* Heathcliff. I shall love mine yet; and take him with me: he's in my
soul" (138). Catherine refuses to mourn the Heathcliff who is not her own
("*my* Heathcliff"), now irretrievably lost, and this "dead" self enters into
Catherine as a subject. Thus the secret self incorporates the desired
other—entombs the beloved in order to keep it for his or her selfish self.
Each is haunted by the other—making each ghostly to him or herself.

Mourning for the beloved is a part of love; in fact, Catherine and
Heathcliff's narrative in *Wuthering Heights* is in love with death. Mournful
love searches for a revenant or any scrap or remainder of the lost beloved:
in *Wuthering Heights* love adheres to scraps, parings, or castoffs.

Heathcliff, in saying good-bye to Catherine just after her death, removes Edgar Linton's pale hair from her locket and replaces it with his own heavy black crop. Heathcliff's hair, as a synecdoche of his material self, symbolically enshrines his body in its most mysterious state: stillness. Here love resides in the decay of the body's ornaments, in its failure, in its always lostness. The body-in-fragments, and in the most fragmentary state—death—comes to represent the possibility of love for Catherine and Heathcliff. [13] That is, it is only in fragments or specters that their love can be, if ever, fulfilled. Throughout the story they describe the way parts of themselves reside in the beloved other. Catherine famously exclaims of Heathcliff, "He is more myself than I am" (68). Upon Catherine's death, Heathcliff calls out in grief: "I *cannot* live without my life! I *cannot* live without my soul!" (144).[14] After her death, he doesn't so much lament that she has gone but rather that he can no longer locate her. "Where is she? Not *there*—not in heaven—not perished—where?" (144). He needs only to find where she now resides. Death does not present a barrier to their love but comes to constitute its very being.

This overarching narrative structure of death can, on a less literal level, be seen in all dangerous lover romances and even, Peter Brooks would argue, is a structure of narrativity itself. As mentioned earlier in relation to the uncanny, the loop in time or the retrograde narrativity of the dangerous lover formula is such that the whole of the story functions in relation to the ending; all of the narrative "happens" because of, or in light of, the end. Heidegger argues that ontology itself is structured in this way. Dasein is not fully completed; it always exists as a potential being until it dies, then all its potential has been used up. Dasein's fundamental make-up involves a stance to temporality that is always ahead of itself—looking forward to the possibilities that it will become; Dasein exists beyond itself. "The not-yet is already included in its own being, by no means as an arbitrary determination, but as a constituent. . . . Dasein is always already its not-yet as long as it is" (*Being and Time*, 244).[15] As soon as there is nothing more "missing," then Dasein will cease to be. Romantic time runs like this as well: at each moment ahead of itself. The moment in the romance arrives both present and potential, now and portent; it is fully here but yet it gazes forward to the immanence of love, the death of the narrative. Each moment moves beyond itself, always a "not-yet" but also always in anticipation of ending. The catching up that happens in the end equals a kind of death, with nothing more "missing." Such "aheadness" serves as an explanation for the hesitant, confused meaning of the sexual encounters in the dangerous lover romance. Because an erotic scene, or any scene, projects itself forward, it runs ahead to its end, and in its very presentness, where all meaning appears complete in the moment, it is also always flavored by the end. The point of full completion of love has its deathlike qualities, as this moment of full meaning happens once, briefly, and when it arrives the romance novel ends. We could say that the romance exhausts itself in plenitude. A sense of a poignant flurry of activity, a restless rush toward the final consumption, runs throughout the narrative. Often a speedy erotic pushes the narrative forward; there is never enough time to have all of the erotic feelings the hero and heroine might. "She wanted to have the time to do her own share of gazing . . . but she couldn't. Quite simply, they didn't have the time. She didn't have the time and the feeling that engulfed her as she saw that he was ready for her turned the whole of her insides to liquid heat" (Jordan, 165). Time is short because the end of the narrative nears, and they must fit in, through intensification, all the love and sex they can. Each scene or potential, secret togetherness is consumed by its relation to the end; every step is saturated by time's fleetingness. The insatiable quality of the romantic temporality exposes the romance's addiction to the other. Addiction races through time, finding only the present of importance and eating through it feverishly. Addicted to each other, the lovers must hurry; they must do it all *right now*. Addiction rushes past death's marker, creating little (and false) infinities along the way.[16] Like all novels, the romance follows Lukács's observation, in his comprehensive theory of the history of the novel, that "we might almost say that the entire inner action of the novel is nothing but a struggle against the power of time" (122). Thus the lovers stave off death by creating little moments of transcendent love, glimmering out of the race toward the end. This consumption of each moment explains why fire and burning desire appear as important symbols to romance. Dorchester Publishers even has a romance series called "Secret Fires." "Wrapping her arms around his neck, she returned his kiss. Fires burned within her, consuming flames that had been a secret even from her" (Rogers, 119). Life is being consumed, used up, by love. "She responded with all the ardor he could have wished for. She burned the cares of the day from him, the troubles of the past, the worries about what tomorrow might hold" (Rogers, 288). The *petit mort,* the little death of the orgasm, brings sex into the realm of danger. Orgasm leads to the possibility of self-dissolution in ecstasy and sublimity, the possibility of burning away all time and being. The secret fire of love will finally burn through to the end of the story, to the end of our hero and heroine.

The poignancy of love in romance comes from the sense that, once the full presence of love arrives, the characters will be gone; they will die to their narrative; there will be nothing left to say. Love becomes a fantasy of dying, a liebestod. Barthes writes that love is a "death liberated from dying" (*Lover's Discourse,* 12). In the classic love story, *Romeo and Juliet,* not only do both the lovers die in the end, for love, but they are doomed as soon as they fall in love, and the play is a slow movement toward death—a play of mourning. The death is their love: love equals death. Nancy writes, "Love offers finitude in its truth; it is finitude's dazzling presentation" (*Inoperative Community*, 99). It is usually a near-death experience that finally brings full confessions or realizations of love in the romance. Death as a possibility illuminates the fragility and mortality of the beloved and the ache of bodily existence.

The link between death and love leads to another manifestation of Heideggerian nearness, the idea of essential being as structured by its relation to death. Heidegger argues, radically, that Dasein can only be understood by looking first at its end. Even the beginning of Dasein must be understood by leading back to it from the end. This convolution of ontology mirrors the narrativity of the dangerous lover formula and, it might be said, any narrativity. When we live in the everyday, we cover over the certainty of death, concealing "that it is possible in every moment" (*Being and Time*, 258). As Heidegger explains, "As soon as a human being is born, he is old enough to die right away" (*Being and Time*, 245).[17] With an authentic stance toward our end, death is understood as always a possibility, an indefinite certainty; Dasein's authenticity toward death is a "holding for true"—is letting this conviction (of the certainty of death) overcome one. This overcoming is a dwelling with the fact that death could come at any moment, which leads to finding Dasein as a whole, as an individuated whole. An authentic being-toward-death does not evade death but makes it Dasein's own as a possibility. A being-toward this possibility does not relate to something actual, but rather it exists "toward" an unknown possibility, which is nevertheless not to be bypassed and belongs uniquely to each Dasein. Hence, existence is at each moment a living with death, a living ready to die, a living always "running ahead" to the end. The structure of this "running ahead" is a way that Dasein is face-to-face with its own self. Dasein is then free to relate to itself as finite. In the shadow of existence's end (death), in the impossibility of existence, Dasein's possibility opens up. Living in the face of death gives Dasein its freedom of possibility.[18]

As soon as a romantic heroine is born, she is old enough to die (fall in love) right away.[19] The series of failures that hold off "dying" are required to make the full presence of love possible. It is out of the continual failure of presence, or the impossibility of existence, that the possibility will come about.[20] The certainty of love (death) often overcomes the heroine; it is an idea always in a relation with essential truth, especially when most evaded, flown from. Every moment of the romance "runs ahead" to the immanence of love at the end. The melancholy ache of dangerous love consists in impossibility illuminating possibility, which gives it its measurelessness. And love, while also being finite, a circumscribable fatality, does lead to a measurelessness at the heart of failure and death. Its boundlessness moves vertically, contained in the moment's intensification and excessiveness, which speeds toward the end. Amorous time is a minute infinity in a moment of loving.

A clear kinship can be traced between Peter Brooks's reading of the relation between narrative and death and Heidegger's concept of an ontological narrativity. Brooks, reading *Beyond the Pleasure Principle,* discusses the implicit narrativity in Freud's theories of desire. Brooks places narrative desire, and the desire for narrative, in the realm of Freud's famous statement, "the aim of all life is death" (quoted in Brooks, 102). The drive to read a plot, Brooks argues, is a death drive, an instinct for an end. Yet the pleasure principle, while desiring the final discharge as well, also postpones the end with various kinds of foreplay, detours, and tensions that will, for a while, hold back the end, or death. Freud's Eros and Thanatos color narrativity with desire and death and make the reading of a novel similar to a sexual experience, with the end a *petit mort.*

The eternity of romance comes in the redemption at the end, the ecstatic, erotic closure: the epiphany. The perfect union has been created, and, in some sense, the end of a romance is the end of all need for romance. Everything arrives solved, beautiful, and complete; everything will be happy from now on. Yet this apparent closure is only apparent; this perfection immediately breaks down into a repetition. The end of the romance leads to the beginning of a new one, which is the meaning of a formulaic genre—that it can be repeated, replicated, again and again. Romance teaches us that love, like philosophy and thinking itself, is never completed. Each declaration of "I love you" is finite and utterly singular, yet in its abundance of meaning, it means both everything and nothing. To say "I love you" points to a singular place and time, with a unique and always changing self that speaks, an "I" and a "you" whose status is always uncertain. In this sense, its meaning is so fleeting; we might say that we can never agree on a meaning for this utterance. Yet, everyone knows what love means; to love is, as Nancy writes, to exist as such: to think, to be, to philosophize. The "I love you" is what can be repeated, perhaps must be repeated. "Love in its singularity, when it is grasped absolutely, is itself perhaps nothing but the indefinite abundance of all possible loves, and an abandonment to their dissemination, indeed to the disorder of these explosions" (*Inoperative Community,* 83). The prodigiousness of the "I love you" is that, while it ends a particular love story, it also stretches beyond it, indicating a future "I love you." Nancy names love as " . . . always the furthest movement of a completion" (*Inoperative Community,* 92). It is not a completion, only a movement of one, a finality opening out to a series of other finalities.

IV. Jane Austen and Sir Walter Scott

Two more pieces of this history need to be put in place at this historical juncture: Austen and Scott. Although played in a subtle key and some-times even discordant to the classic tune, many of Austen's novels are part of the history of seduction narratives, of the reformed rake genre, of the gothic romance even. Scott's novels also hold these themes, and he was particularly interested in Gothic villains and the enemy/lover. *Sense and Sensibility*'s (1811) seduction narrative qualities stand out when set in this light, although the seduction is abandoned when only partially achieved. Willoughby takes the role of rake, living beyond his means, recklessly playing with Marianne's affections and then betraying her. Yet Willoughby does not have the hidden demeanor or the dark interior of a dangerous lover; in fact, he is generally an open, affectionate man who has simply gone wrong; as Elinor muses: her "thoughts were silently fixed on the irreparable injury which too early an independence and its consequent habits of idleness, dissipation, and luxury, had made in [his] mind, [his] character, [his] happiness . . . the world has made him extravagant and vain. Extravagance and vanity had made him coldhearted and selfish" (287). Largely redeemed in the end, at least in the eyes of Elinor, Willoughby does not quite fit into the reformed rake formula because his power as a driver of the narrative scatters in his mercenary marriage, tak-ing him largely outside the lives of the characters central to the book. *Sense and Sensibility* falls into the didactic category of romance while the gothic romance is generally an amorous type. In the gothic romance the guilt of the hero only increases the hero's magnetism, whereas in Austen his attraction wanes when his guilt is starkly rendered as true. For instance, in *Rebecca,* the discovery that Max murders his first wife only makes him more attractive to the heroine. Willoughby, never so villain-ous, is punished when he doesn't get Marianne and is doomed in the end to feel his loss sharply. Darcy of *Pride and Prejudice* (1813) influenced the creation of many later dangerous lover figures in his powerfully aloof stance as the rich misanthrope who stands apart, sneering at the vanity and silly folly of those around him.[21] Darcy is proud, a snob in fact, and the plot's movement is driven by the need to humble Darcy so that he will realize the worth of the middle-class Elizabeth. While Darcy's only vio-lence lies in his reserve, his resentfulness, on some level he becomes a rake who must be reformed. This drawing-room Cinderella story, like *Jane*

Eyre and *Pamela,* is an important point of origin for the "rags to riches" theme in contemporary romance. The dangerous lover's redemption lies also in love overpowering considerations of class. Clearly class *does* matter to the heroine because an important part of the story—often a fantasy of romance and we can see this in the twentieth century with *Rebecca*—is not only to have the man, his love, but also to share his power, meaning his capital.

Other signs of the dangerous lover in Austen cluster around Captain Benwick in *Persuasion* (1818), who is proud of his "melancholy air" and mourns for his dead fiancée. He reads Byron's *The Bride of Abydos* and *The Giaour,* and identifies with their heroes closely: "he showed himself so intimately acquainted with . . . all the impassioned descriptions of hopeless agony . . . he repeated, with such tremulous feeling, the various lines which imagined a broken heart, or a mind destroyed by wretchedness" (100). But Benwick's poetical, aesthetic melancholy is not taken seriously, becoming only a weakness of disposition. With Benwick and *Northanger Abbey,* Austen pokes fun at the passions of the Gothic hero/villain.

One of Scott's important contributions to the dangerous lover narrative is his strong sense of the nostalgia of love and its connection to a great past, now irrevocably lost. Important to later historical fiction, Scott's historical romances express the secret reaches of the vast, mysterious, mythical past, and its ancient magic and folklore. Scott made history itself the adventure of the individual in a world obscured by the depths of time. His characters themselves, including his dangerous heroes, become mythical. In *The Bride of Lammermore* (1819), Scottish myth creates the doom-destined hero, whose love and life are fated to end horribly from the very start. The movement of the story has the complex narrativity of a recounting of events about lovers who are, in some sense, already dead, both because the narrator tells us from the beginning of their imminent fate, but also because myth has already accounted for their lives and their dreadful end. The house and name of Ravenswood is cursed to decay, and the current master lives in poverty. The narrative begins with Ravenswood's melancholy brooding: "But its space was peopled by phantoms which the imagination of the young heir [Ravenswood] conjured up before him—the tarnished honor and degraded fortunes of his house, the destruction of his own hopes, and the triumph of that family by whom they had been ruined. To a mind naturally of a gloomy cast here was ample room for meditation" (22). An ancient legend, obscured and garbled by temporal distance, tells of the death of the last of the Ravenswood race. His death is linked by legend to the death of his beloved, who will die of her love for him. The tragedy of the myth begins its inexorable course when Edgar Ravenswood meets

Lucy Ashton, the daughter of his sworn enemy, at a fountain known by legend to be fatal to the Ravenswood family. Lucy Ashton falls in love with the hero largely because of the pain inscribed on his brow: "Some sweet sorrow, or the brooding spirit of some moody passion, had quenched the light and ingenuous vivacity . . . and it was not easy to gaze on the stranger without a secret impression either of pity or awe" (45). Our lovers appear ghostly from the start, and the Byronic Master of Ravenswood, "with dark and sullen brow" (21), has his gloomy death written all over his countenance. Ravenswood does not develop into a rounded character; his countenance in some sense *is* his character. Ravenswood's gloominess is never cast off, the weight of myth and superstition hound him to his tragic end.

While Ravenswood's passion and willfulness give him a powerful mien and deportment, his actions only pull him deeper and deeper into his foretold doom. Many of Scott's heroes appear very modern in their passivity and their languishing attitude toward the tragedy of fate. Alexander Welsh defines two kinds of heroes in Scott—the passive and the dark one. The passive hero, such as Nigel in *The Fortunes of Nigel,* finds himself "a victim of events": "whatever of good or bad has befallen me, hath arisen out of the agency of others, not from my own" (quoted in Welsh, 32). Ravenswood, although passionate, takes very little decided action against his fate. He does initially save the heroine from death, but this brings about their love, which begins the legend that will end in death. He blusters into the scene at the climax of the book, when Lucy is being forced to marry another, and threatens violence, but his actions only serve to foreground his inability to counter his already written story. Ravenswood's passionate defeat, his feeling of lostness in the hands of a harsh world, point forward to the hero of the erotic historical.

Scott's "dark" hero, as Welsh defines him, usually moves outside the law; "he acts with deep feeling, and his intentions are 'good,' though fierce and mistaken" (59). George Staunton of *The Heart of Mid-Lothian* (1818) is just such a figure. While Staunton comes of very good family—eventually he becomes Sir Staunton—in his youth he leaves his home; rebels against his religious father; and becomes a smuggler, a robber, and a vigilante. He seduces and impregnates two women, one who goes mad after her mother murders her child, and the other who is almost hanged for the apparent death of her child. He has the vices of many dangerous heroes: "He was so well acquainted with the turf, the gaming-table, the cock-pit, and every worse rendezvous of folly and dissipation, that his mother's fortune was spent before he was twenty-one, and he was soon in debt and distress" (358). Yet there is something about his very willfulness, his passion, and the depths of his despair that make him romantic. Staunton's manner is "daring and unrestrained," his carriage "bold and somewhat superfluous" (111). He is described by Butler, the clergyman:

> The fiery eye, the abrupt demeanor, the occasionally harsh, yet studiously subdued tone of voice,—the features, handsome, but now clouded with pride, now disturbed by suspicion, now inflamed by passion—the dark hazel eyes which he sometimes shaded with his cap, as if he were averse to have them seen while they were occupied with keenly observing the motions and bearings of others—those eyes that were now turbid with melancholy, now gleaming with scorn, and now sparkling with fury—was it the passions of a mere mortal they expressed, or the emotions of a fiend, who seeks, and seeks in vain, to conceal his fiendish designs under the borrowed mask of manly beauty? The whole partook of the mein, language, and port of the ruined archangel. (115)

His show of passion is so extreme he appears to be a Lucifer or some kind of non-human demon. His remorse for past deeds consumes him: "Think what it is, to rush uncalled unto the presence of an offended Deity, your heart fermenting with evil passions, your hand hot from the steel you have been urging, with your best skill and malice, against the breast of a fellow-creature. Or, suppose yourself the scarce less wretched survivor, with the guilt of Cain, the first murderer, in your heart, with his stamp upon your brow" (113). To see Staunton as a Cain-like figure is to disclose his kinship with the ever-wandering Byronic hero. The hero of the erotic historical also carries the burden of restless wandering, of depthless passions that remained unslaked until the heroine appears. Yet Staunton does marry his beloved, and he is reconciled to his father and hence his fortune, but instead of being redeemed, soothed, and happy with his lot, he still manages to pine. His "gloomy thoughts make him terrible to himself and others" (475) and the compulsion to hide his passions in order to maintain his position in society lead him to "consume his health, destroy his temper, and render him at once an object of dread and compassion" (521). Staunton finds no quietude on this earth.

In Scott's *The Pirate* (1822), one of his most Gothic novels, love reaches into the obscure depth of time, becomes material in dangerous cliffs, the uncontrollable storm, the wind-foamed sea. The dark sublime bounds subjectivity in nature's ravenous dangers and an ineffable destiny.

'Tis not alone the scene; the man, Anselmo,
The man finds sympathies in these wild wastes

And roughly tumbling seas, which fairer views
And smoother waves deny him. (Scott, 22)

The Pirate is a novel-length version of Byron's *The Corsair*. Scott quotes from Byron's poem to describe his corsair, Captain Cleveland, one of Welsh's dark heroes. Cleveland has a "spirit so unsettled and stormy, whose life has hitherto been led in scenes of death and peril" (251). Like a true dangerous lover, his name is "as terrible as a tornado" (276) and his face has become an "iron mask." Not long after Cleveland washes up on the shores of Zetland, the rocky, wind and sea-tossed setting of the novel, he searches for expiation for his violent, outlawed life, so that he may be redeemed and marry his beloved, Minna. Like a Byronic hero, Cleveland ultimately fails to be united with his beloved, but he does give up his life of rape and pillage and becomes a worthy soldier, fighting for his country. *The Pirate* recounts an erotic scene which later becomes dear to the erotic historical: the story of the pirate who captures the heroine and makes her his love slave (although Scott only alludes to the chance of Minna taking this role).[22]

As the next chapter recounts, Byronism and its infinite longings, its tormented sense of homelessness, come out of Scott, among other places, and particularly Scott's ideals of nostalgia and the vast sweep of myth and the past. Scott's dangerous lovers were dark rovers who hid secret crimes, who couldn't find a spiritual home on this earth, who were doomed before their story ever started.

CHAPTER THREE

Love as Homesickness

Longing for a Transcendental Home in Byron and the Brontës (1811–1847)

We have eaten from the tree of knowledge. Now paradise is bolted shut, and the angel stands behind us. We must journey around the world and see whether perhaps it is open again somewhere on the yonder side.
—Heinrich von Kleist

In his essay on the uncanny, Freud mentions briefly what he calls a humorous saying: "Love is homesickness" (399). He goes on to connect this to homesickness for the mother's womb, which manifests itself in the uncanniness of the female genitalia. But a more simple reading of this expression also generates meaning: the nostalgia of falling in love. Nostalgia comes from the Greek "nostos" for "return home" and "algia" for pain. The OED defines it as "a form of melancholia caused by prolonged absence from one's home or country or a severe homesickness." Another interpretation of the etymology of this word, however, implies that the nostalgia or sickness comes from a return home, a return to a home that is changed from the passing of time—that is no longer the ideal home of memory. Love, then, opens the doors of memory, of childhood familiarities and happiness; hence, love accesses the desire to go back to a past that, because closed by time, resides in the rosy light of a lost paradise. Love leads to homesickness because its ideal quality illuminates the impossibility of other ideals, those tied to the belongingness of the past—the childhood haunts, the home country.[1] Yet another way to read this expression turns on understanding the amorous attraction of one who is homeless; it elucidates the tendency to fall in love with the pathologically homesick. The eroticism of homesickness settles around the desire for one who restlessly pines; who searches always for something long gone; who, in a word, desires. Here we step into the realm where love partakes of the outside, where love describes a

48

desire to be with, or to be oneself, an outsider. And the home stands as an important trope for many love narratives, where homesickness becomes both literal and figural with the fugitive, melancholy wayfarer, who is both loved and loves under the sign of his homesickness. The legacy of Byronism in fiction includes linked concepts of existence and love that are based upon an erotics of homesickness. The question presses: Why does the mark of Cain become a mark of the beloved?

I. The Erotic Wanderer

The figure of the tortured hero created by Byron stands as an early articulation of ideas central to Modernism, such as Georges Lukács's theory of the transcendentally homeless—the lack of and need for a home wherein a belief in a true and fixed meaning can be housed, such as God or Nature. Byron's figure of the traveler stands also as a prototype for such influential theories of subjectivity as the world-weary, world-traveled, sophisticated Aesthete of Oscar Wilde and the philosophers of the late Victorian journal *The Yellow Book*, whose jaded palates seek ever-newer scenes to whet their appetites. Related also to the flâneur in Proust, Baudelaire, and Benjamin, Childe Harold's voyages mark him as a connoisseur of human nature, an idler whose work is to brood.

Beginning with Childe Harold's poetical voyage around the world, the Byronic figure eroticizes the voyager so important to the imagination of Western culture,[2] linking him to a tradition that stretches back to Odysseus as the lost traveler, looking for his homeland.[3] The mythic *liebestod* lover, Shakespeare's Romeo, whose name means "roamer," or "wanderer," marks the tie between love and travel. *Romeo and Juliet,* riddled with metaphors of pilgrimage and sea voyaging, pictures lovesickness leading to a melancholy end. Love's destiny, fated from the start, encompasses an itinerary that travels the wide ocean. Romeo versifies to Juliet:

> I am no pilot, yet wert thou as far,
> As that vast shore wash'd with the farthest sea,
> I should adventure for such merchandise. (2.2.87–89)

The Byronic hero, particularly the Giaour and Childe Harold, roams disenchanted and always astray; he has no place in the domesticity of society. Different from the flâneur and the Aesthete, however, Childe Harold circles the earth in passionate torment, a ruined vagabond. Doomed to lorn voyaging, he searches, always failing, to be *placed,* comfortable, situated in a context that fits. Not just aloof, the Byronic hero often, like the Giaour and the Corsair, is a criminal, an outlaw who is not only self-exiled, but who also actively, hatefully works against society, as a murderous pirate or a vengeful lover. Outside the law of society, also cast out of a heaven or paradise, he moves with the likes of Lucifer, Cain, the Wandering Jew, and the Flying Dutchman, all popular figures in numerous Gothic novels, as well as other Romantic poetry.[4] The Wandering Jew, Ahasuerus from medieval legend, was an infidel who cursed Christ at the crucifixion. For this heresy, he was made to wander the earth, until the Second Coming, seeking death and peace. Byron's Manfred and the Giaour feel they have profoundly sinned, it doesn't matter how or why, and they are cursed with the pains of remorse, not only for their crimes but also for their self-inflicted homelessness.[5] Redemption for these characters will come only with death, unless forgetfulness or madness are possibilities. Childe Harold compares himself to the Wandering Jew: "It is that settled, ceaseless gloom / The fabled Hebrew Wanderer bore; / That will not look beyond the tomb, / But cannot hope for rest before" (1.86.26–29). And Manfred also wants to forget his crime through self-oblivion:

> . . .—I have prayed
> For madness as a blessing—'tis denied me.
> I have affronted Death—but in the war
> Of elements the waters shrunk from me,
> And fatal things passed harmless; the cold hand
> Of an all-pitiless Demon held me back,
> Back by a single hair, which would not break.
> . . . I dwell in my despair—
> And live—and live for ever. (2.2.134–48)

Caught in gigantism, Manfred's capacity to think and suffer is so immense, it is almost immortal, even superhuman.

The other possibility of redemption for Byronic dislocation is, of course, finding a home in the beloved. Byron's unique manifestation of the myth of the wandering and outcast hero brings homelessness into a narrative of love by delineating it as a melancholy chaos that might possibly be ordered or bounded through a second self. Love might give the terrible internalized infinite of his desire a home. Among the many myths that feed this erotic legend is the Flying Dutchman.[6] The basic outline of his story begins with the Captain vowing he will round the Cape of Good Hope during a heavy storm, or be damned. Some versions more explicitly state that he makes a pact with the devil: if his ship makes the Cape he will give up his soul to eternal damnation. When the Flying Dutchman succeeds in this voyage, he becomes cursed by Satan to sail the seas forever. Wagner's famous version of this legend, first performed in 1843, comes from Heinrich Heine's novel of the 1830s, *From the Memoirs of Herr von Schnabelewopski*. The Flying Dutchman, called by Heine "the Wandering Jew of the ocean," feels "agony as deep as the sea on which he sails" (100). Forever doomed to be exiled from a native land, imprisoned on his enchanted ship, he despairs in his homelessness. Heine writes a new resolution of the story—the possibility of redemption for the Captain by the love of a woman. The devil has no faith in a woman's "truth" (sexual fidelity) and hence gives the Flying Dutchman the chance to arrive at port every seven years and attempt to meet a faithful woman; such a success will lead to the salvation of his soul. He does meet a woman who falls in love with him, and she agrees to sail the seas with him, hence herself becoming an outcast. But the Flying Dutchman, in his love for her and his desire to save her from having to live in his curse, leaves without her. In the tragic end, affirming she will be true to him, she throws herself off a cliff into the sea. In her desperate act of final abandonment to love (and to death), she binds the Flying Dutchman to the desolating round of no true abode; he is saved yet never saved—the curse dissolves yet he has lost his true love.

The lover as a figure for redemption is a common trope in Byron. The Byronic figure's one beloved, who for the Corsair is Medora, Manfred Astarte, the Giaour Leila, and Childe Harold an unspecified woman, is represented as a container for the purest good and the highest truth. She could bring a final presentness, a transfiguration, a blessed grace.[7] The Giaour states, "She was my Life's unerring Light: / That quenched—what beam shall break my night?" (1145–46). Hence homelessness seems possibly surmountable by discovering a location for the essential being in another, in a two-person subjectivity. The Corsair's love is described:

> Yes—it was Love—if thoughts of tenderness,
> Tried by temptation, strengthened by distress,
> Unmoved by absence, firm in every clime,
> And yet—Oh more than all!—untired by Time;
> Which nor defeated hope, nor baffled wile,
> Could render sullen were She to smile. . . . (1.293–98)

Love creates a dwelling place in space and time, filling it up so that it becomes reachable, permeable, pliable. One of the most obvious reasons for the appropriation of the Byronic figure by love narratives and romance is the Byronic hero's sweeping belief in the possibility of love as the most important force for defining being itself, and for locating the transcendental home.

But heaven itself descends in Love;
A feeling from the Godhead caught,
To wean from self each sordid thought;
A ray of Him who formed the whole;
A Glory circling round the soul! *(The Giaour,* 1136–40)

The Byronic philosophy sees love as the ultimate, and only, essential truth and final resting place for one in this life. Love is the only force that still holds meaning.

The Brontë children were fascinated by Byron's dashing life and his damned characters; he figures heavily in the juvenilia of Charlotte, Branwell, and Emily.[8] They were mesmerized by the sheer impossibility of his being: his existence based on love, yet his love always impossible. The very foundations of love for the Byronic hero are based on failure and the forgetting of what is possible. The Byronic hero in his purity can, by definition, never be redeemed by becoming a couple, he is interminably thrown back upon black despair; he is unremittingly cast adrift into absence and dark night. In *The Corsair,* Conrad loses Medora because she pines away when she thinks he is dead. In *The Giaour,* Leila is murdered by her master because of her love for the Giaour, and the Giaour's life becomes one of vengeance against her murderer and then a tortured living in the past of his love. In *Manfred,* Astarte has died because of his unspecified sin. But finally the hero fails because this is the definition of the Byronic hero. He is the tormented melancholy failure who nears success and then fails and experiences the eternal loss, the repetition of the impossibility of bliss.[9] He retains his status as the outcast, the dangerous lover whose subjectivity is as large and as impoverished as the world. For Jane Eyre and innumerable other romantic heroines (and heroes), to become an ideal lover, to turn this impoverished world into a plenitude, is to obtain an impossibility. To make the impossible possible is the erotic excitement of the dangerous lover romance.

Directly descended from the Byronic hero, Rochester in *Jane Eyre* and Heathcliff in *Wuthering Heights* exemplify beloved, estranged waifs.[10] Rochester explains to Jane how, after his hated wife went mad and he discovered the lies of his father and brother, he became lost to himself, belonged only to the foreign, to the outside which knows no intimacy.

I transformed myself into a Will-o'-the-wisp. . . . I pursued wanderings as wild as those of the Marsh spirit. I sought the Continent, and went devious through all its Lands. . . . Disappointment made me reckless. I tried dissipation . . . in a harsh, bitter frame of mind, the result of a useless, roving, lonely life—corroded with disappointment, sourly disposed against all men. . . . (348–51)

Rochester's superior, misanthropic pain projects his bitter mind onto the world; by desperate roaming he tries to outrun this lack of belief in any possibility of a "home." Heathcliff, as a young child, is "dark almost as if it [he] came from the devil" (36). He is a "gypsy brat" who was discovered "starving, houseless, and as good as dumb in the streets of Liverpool" (37). A vagabond, an "out and outer," he haunts the thresholds of the Earnshaw family, first as a replacement for Mr. Earnshaw's dead son, then as an abused "servant" by Hindley after Mr. Earnshaw's death. With his rough, brutal, demonlike appearance and actions, he lurks around the margins of society. Insidious to family unity, to the couple, he is described by Catherine, after he returns from his three years of mysterious roaming, in this way, " . . . Heathcliff is an unreclaimed creature, without refinement— without cultivation; an arid wilderness of furze and whinstone" (101). Blighting both interiority and exteriority, his subjectivity, like the desolate moors, desiccates all around him.

Cain remains the exemplary figure for desolate homelessness. Byron identified personally with Cain's curse, and many of his created characters have ties to various aspects of the Cain myth. Cain carries the mark of his sin for killing Abel, and he must be forever an exiled traveler as expiation for this sin. Besides his drama titled *Cain,* Byron portrays Childe Harold seeing himself like Cain: " . . . life-abhorring Gloom / Wrote on his faded brow curst Cain's unresting doom" (1.73.8–9). His gloom will not rest; it stings him into more and more restless roving, ceaseless thinking. He cannot outrun his remorse as much as he tries. And in *The Giaour,* the hero condemns himself for Leila's death: "She died—I dare not tell thee how; / But look—'tis written on my brow!" (1057–58). The Byronic figure is *marked* as a fugitive; his homelessness can be seen on his face. His sin is sometimes so primal, or so profound, that it becomes merely a cipher, or even unspeakable. Like Coleridge's Ancient Mariner who must wander in expiation for killing the Albatross: " . . . this soul hath been / Alone on a wide wide sea: / So lonely 'twas, that God himself / Scarce seemed there to be" (597–600) and whose sin and punishment are marked by his eye fixing his audience in horror so that they must listen to his tale, the Byronic figure's lonely soul, while withdrawn from other men, human communities, values, a God, needs to be witnessed. He desires to have someone to hear his story, to *see* his depths of pain. Byron's interest in Cain lies in this paradox: his sin and pain is so primal it is almost unrepresentable, yet it is unmistakably written on his face.

The deeply unhappy, estranged brooder, with outward signs of the darkness that is inside him, has become a ubiquitous trope for the dangerous lover narrative.[11] Rochester's scarred face after the fire of Thornfield signifies his lived punishment but also his exiled status; Jane's love is his only redemption in life. Melville's Captain Ahab carries his obsessive, wayfaring pain on his face; all who see him know he is cursed to wander. The "enemy lover" or "demon lover's" dark frown, his tortured and furrowed brow magnetically draw those around him. In Bulwer-Lytton's *Pelham,* Sir Reginald Glanville, a beautiful, brilliant man whose seduction and inadvertent destruction of a middle-class girl lays waste to his life, is consumed with remorse and obsessed with revenge. His countenance marks his tortured subjectivity, "a gloom and despondency which seemed almost like aberration of intellect . . . his cheek was hollow and hueless, his eye dim, and of that visionary and glassy aspect . . . which, according to the superstitions of some nations, implies a mysterious and unearthly communion of the soul with the beings of another world" (176). As a worshipper of sorrow and a man whose salvation is lost as soon as his narrative begins, he is compared to a kind of circle: " . . . a circle can only touch a circle in one place, everything that life presents to him, wherever it comes from, to whatever portion of his soul it is applied, can find but one point of contact; and that is the soreness of affliction: whether it is the *oblivio* or the *otium* that he requires, he finds equally that he is forever in want of one treasure" (177). In Trollope's *Can You Forgive Her?* the attractive, villainous rake, George Vavasor, receives a knife wound to his face in a violent scuffle as a boy. While outwardly a suave and persuasive gentleman, inside his nature is dark and violent. The scar tells us this from the start, but his violence doesn't explicitly show itself until the end of the story. "On some occasions, when he was angry or disappointed, it was very hideous; for he would so contort his face that the scar would, as it were, stretch itself out, revealing all its horrors, and his countenance would become all scar" (32). Unredeemably cursed like Cain, he becomes a voyager in the end, sailing for America to escape punishment for his murderous actions. Thackeray's *Vanity Fair* includes the blue-blooded "prince" Lord Steyne who, although famous for his worldly carelessness, his cruel misanthropy, and his excessive dissipation, falls for Becky. When Becky's husband, Colonel Crawley, discovers Steyne and Becky alone in intimate conversation and flirtation, he rips Steyne's gift of a diamond ornament off Becky's chest and casts it at Steyne, cutting his forehead. "The scar cut by the diamond on his white, bald, shining forehead, made a burning red mark" (630). Lord Steyne has always felt cursed because of an inherited susceptibility to madness, and his scar signifies a kind of deadness to life, along with his "livid face and ghastly eyes . . . ordinarily they gave no light and seemed tired of looking out on a world of which almost all the pleasure and all the best beauty had palled upon the worn-out wicked old man" (632).

Childe Harold wanders not only because of his sin and his misanthropy—his ideals too pure to be sullied by the common race of men—

but most importantly, he wanders to escape his own consciousness. Hence, his self-exile leads to the question, "What Exile from himself can flee?" (1.74.30). He is "the wandering outlaw of his own dark mind" (3.3.2). Here we must pay particular attention to the fact that, unlike Cain, the Wandering Jew, and the Ancient Mariner, the Byronic hero is self-exiled. This modern trait connects him to the alienation of the artist we find with Joyce, Stein, Faulkner, and Kafka. Even though Cain and the Wandering Jew act willfully so that wandering is their punishment, there is no sense that they can choose redemption—be accepted back into the fold. Yet the Byronic hero *might* be able to find redemption because his exile is situated in his own mind. His self-exile links him to Milton's Satan, who has created his own hell in his mind. When the spirits speak to Manfred—"By thy delight in others' pain, / And by thy brotherhood of Cain, / I call upon thee! And compel / Thyself to be thy proper Hell!" (1.1.248–52)—Milton's Satan in *Paradise Lost* seems to be speaking his famous lines: "Which way I fly is Hell; myself am Hell" (4.75). But even for Satan there are exterior forces at work (God) that deny him entrance back into the heavenly fold. The Byronic hero, by contrast, acts, at each moment, on his own free will. This existential abyss of personal choice is why Nietzsche preferred Byron's Faustian Manfred to Goethe's Faust. Unlike Faust, Manfred stands alone; he does not even give the devil his due.[12] His subjectivity becomes entirely his own.

The Byronic self complicates the division between subjectivity's interior and exterior. Related to the Romantic sublime, his subjectivity lacks liminals; it is boundless.[13] One reason why the Byronic hero exiles himself from society is that his consciousness creates the world as a mirror of his own hellish mind; the world is an interior space where all is bereft of meaning. He restlessly circles this world of his own making, this infinite mindscape. The world can provide no relief or change because of the immutable script in his mind.

> Alike all time, abhorred all place,
> Shuddering I shrank from Nature's face,
> Where every hue the charmed before
> The blackness of my bosom wore. (*The Giaour,* 1196–1200)

His thoughts taint "all time," "all place," and make all of Nature black like his own heart. The Byronic figure's hell is situated in memory; it is because he cannot forget the past that he is imprisoned in a soul tormented by remorse. In some sense, he has lost the possibility of the present as an ever-changing, moving scene, containing the possibility of change because of his moral fixity on a point in the past that will not pass. Manfred states,

" . . . and for / The future, till the past be gulfed in darkness, / It is not of
my search" (1.2.5–7). The past negates temporality; the only way he can fall
back into time is if the past is obliterated, "gulfed in darkness." He is lost in
a self-perpetuating agony that comes from an idealization of a past
"before"—"before" his fall from grace, "before" his realization of the vanity
and valuelessness of human society. The Byronic hero feels he once had a
home in this world before he realized his desires were so profound they
could never be fulfilled in this life. He imagines that, in the past, he lived in
a world full of immanent meaning, where his desires for ideals such as Truth,
Beauty, and Purity were still in play, still open as possibilities. Yet from the
beginning of *Childe Harold, The Giaour,* and *Manfred,* the Byronic hero is
always already unredeemable. The past can never be passed. The Byronic
hero's homesick wandering is interminable because he cannot absent himself from time, from those aspects of life which make people mortal, earth-
bound; yet he also feels himself cast out of a present and future temporality,
an interest and place in a country, a people, a community.

For the Byronic hero, the tragedy already happens before the story
begins. Barthes explains that love is not narrative: "For me, on the contrary, this story has *already taken place;* for what is event is exclusively the
delight of which I have been the object and whose after effects I repeat
(and fail to achieve) . . . amorous seduction takes place before discourse"
(*Lover's Discourse,* 93–94; emphasis in original). Jock Mcleod, in his discussion of Canto Three of *Childe Harold* and Byron himself in his letters,
refers to the narrator as "coming after." For the dangerous lover, time is
always out of joint: " . . . in love, the truth always comes too late"
(Deleuze, *Proust,* 86).[14] In the time of the dangerous lover, it is always too
late: to find grace, to be an idealistic youth, to believe, to have faith, to
find true love again, to live in the present moment. The temporal structure of the too-late closes off the present and the future. Because meaning is already past, time does not pass; the past is the only time of possibility and because it can never be retrieved, relived, time fails. In too-lateness lies the inability to forget, to forgive oneself and others. In
Middlemarch (1871), Will Ladislaw's diluted Byronism brings to him "a
pouting air of discontent" (52). Mr. Brooke comments that he "may turn
out a Byron . . ." (55).[15] When he thinks that he cannot have Dorothea's
love, he shows a Byronic sense of the "too-late": "There are certain things
which a man can only go through once in his life; and he must know
some time or other that the best is over with him" (437). His lostness is
appeased when he finds a home in his love for Dorothea; she comes to
represent all of truth, purity, and goodness. Will feels, when in Dorothea's
presence, that his "love is satisfied in the completeness of the beloved
object" (251). Will's reformation, his domestication through his love for

Dorothea, lead him to become a responsible citizen, a hardworking politician. Sidney Carton, the "careless and slovenly if not debauched" (135) immoral ruin in Dickens's *A Tale of Two Cities,* also lives in the Byronic world of too-lateness: "It is too late for that. I shall never be better than I am. I shall sink lower and be worse" (229). He always wishes to go back to a "before time": a time before he became a drunk, before he descended "the cloud of caring for nothing." This "cloud" "overshadowed him with such a fatal darkness, [and] was very rarely pierced by the light within him" (228). He comments about himself, "I am like one who died young. All my life might have been" (230).

As a wanderer whose subjectivity includes the whole world—eternal space—the Byronic hero also occludes time in his ownership of infinity. He has lived ages, an eternity, even though he is still young. He has experienced more in his short life than most will in a whole long life. Byron describes a moment of the Giaour's life:

> But in that instant o'er his soul
> Winters of Memory seem to roll,
> And gather in that drop of time
> A life of pain, an age of crime. . . .
> Though in Time's record nearly nought,
> It was Eternity to Thought!
> For infinite as boundless space
> The thought that Conscience must embrace,
> Which in itself can comprehend
> Woe without name, or hope, or end. (261–76)

Byronic mind-time is a momentary intensification in which an eternity is lived, or an infinity of space is realized. As the eternal or infinite are not dwelling places where familiarity is encountered—where final beliefs are housed, where fixed truths are discoverable—time and space themselves lead to the disenchantment of the abodeless. Because the Byronic subjectivity is unbounded, containing everything, he can decimate all of it, hence dwelling in and interiorizing nothingness in all its vastness. The Byronic impairment of the fabric of time takes his story into the mythic realm, a transcendental outside where the cessation of time, of the self, is desired, exhaustedly and from the start.

Imprisoned in its thoughts, the Byronic mind alienates the man, the subject, from the world, from moving time, from presence. This figure, attempting to reconcile the relationship of his mind and the world, becomes the intellectual of Novalis's expression: "Philosophy is actually homesickness—the urge to be everywhere at home" (135).[16] The Byronic brooder has this urge, which explains his ceaseless roving, his desire for the highest ideals, the purest truths.[17] The Byronic figure can be seen as emblematic of the constellation of ideas put forth by the German Romantics who wrote on the problematic possibility of the "modern" self being unified and of this self having and living a meaningful connectedness with the "external" world. Heathcliff explains, "My mind is so eternally secluded in itself" (320). Abrams, in his *Natural Supernaturalism*, explores the use of the trope of the journey and a sickness for home in the German Romantics' ideas on consciousness. Focusing on Schiller, Abrams traces the theory of the journey of the individual from an originary self-unity, a home, through a complex self-consciousness that involves seeing the self as an object and then reaching for a higher unity, which is, however, never quite attainable. This is precisely what Hegel later calls his dialectic, which is the movement of consciousness from an initial alienation, to a transcending of this objectification of the self, which leads, finally, to a synthesis wherein the self finds a home in his/her otherness. The eternal wandering of the Byronic hero occupies a more radical, skeptical, and hence more modern space; it breaks the Hegelian dialectical circle.[18] With Byronism the spirit does not become alienated so that it can find itself again as an absolute goal; rather, it becomes alienated and its meaning comes from this alienation and the always failed attempt to return to this lost home of unity. Mcleod discusses a similar concept of Byronic desire which he describes as metaphysical; that is, desire for distance between subject and object. "Byron's desire, then, is to be so separated from the object that he can imagine conjunction with it" (269).

The subjectivity of the lost wanderer is more closely related to the Kantian crises—what Kant himself called his "Copernican Revolution" or "transcendental idealism"—an important point in philosophy with which all the German Romantics wrestled. Kant was the first to see space and time grounded in the experiencing subject. The "thing in itself" became totally unknowable to the subject because the thing must always be filtered through our sense of time and space—forms of our sensibility with which we perceive the world. Thus the Kantian crisis constructs the subject as one whose experience must always be mediated. Friedrich Hölderlin sees this loss of immediacy as the definition of tragedy—the tragedy of the speculative. Hölderlin feels that the essence of tragedy is that we can never have immediate experience, that as soon as we think we have always already lost immediacy. Therefore, the subject thinks to bring the object of thought closer, through knowledge, but this attempt to bring closer always causes the "thing" to withdraw. Hölderlin was continually working, primarily through his poetry, to close up the Kantian "wound," although he was tortured by the final impossibility of this task. The

Byronic figure's tragedy, similarly, is that consciousness itself always brings solitary wandering, loss of immediacy, loss of presence. The philosophy of the Byronic hero contains a desire for the world to contain his ideals, to fulfill his longing, and he brings the whole world into play and sets it in relation to his thoughts, his consciousness. But because he fails, the relationship between the traveled world and the mind does not bring a sense of the "whole," but rather of the irrevocably lost.[19] The lostness does not belittle the world, however, but makes it eternal and infinite, and hence its ravaged emptiness sets up an infinite longing rather than indifference.

II. Homelessness as Escape

But perhaps maintaining a state of self-alienation, of never finding the final synthesis that Hegel defines as the highest moment of his dialect, can be seen as an escape. The radical outside of the dialectic could be a new-found freedom, albeit on the edge of possibility. Living in every way just on the edge—of oblivion, of insanity, of death—the Byronic figure creates a realm of escape, an outside where the pains of living become so mythical and immense that subjectivity may dissolve at any moment. Everyday difficulties are no worry to such a sublimely tormented well of selfhood; the existential edge lies so close, failure is on such a large scale, it hardly matters anymore. It is in the freedom to be passionately tormented that the attraction for the heroine of a Rochester or Heathcliff can be located. There are numerous points of sublime torture in Byronic love narratives that take on the character of flight from the everyday round: intense study, insomnia, anorexia, autoeroticism. Another is being somehow outside the pale of the family. Manfred's escape from the father comes from being hardly mortal, therefore not subject to the laws of the father, yet not himself a god or father. "But we, who name ourselves its sovereigns, we, / Half dust, half deity, alike unfit / To sink or soar" (1.2.39–41). Manfred's inbetweenness—his unfitness—creates "a line of escape," as Deleuze would call it; homelessness traces a way out. Deleuze and Guattari explore escaping as not so much a movement in any particular direction, but rather a "flight of intensity," the ability to go "head over heels and away" (6). This intense flight "signifies," or takes on the form of a representation, as little as possible; it "breaks the symbolic structure" (7).

The pallid thinker, the intellectual, and the student: many Byronic heroes, most famously Manfred and such Romantic and Gothic Fausts as Melmoth and Victor Frankenstein (whom Mary Shelley modeled after Percy Bysshe, himself a studier of the occult), study late into the night. They study to gain Adam and Eve's forbidden knowledge, the kind that will bring them closer to the gods, that will raise them up above a society for which they feel no fitness. They study at night to define their work hours differently than daytime industry. Nocturnal research serves to move them outside of the social code; their knowledge does not seek to inform, to be disseminated, but rather they study to hoard, to collect and acquire what is generally not believed in, or is thought to be evil, perverse, against what is good and right. This "wrong" knowledge, a subterranean magic, dream knowledge, burrows into the depths of that which can never be fully known or owned. The accumulation of knowledge without discipline, without an end of action, of scholarly merit, is to fall, like Eve, from the grace of properly bounded thought which illuminates, elucidates. In the rebellious stance of his fall the dangerous lover gathers a Luciferian darkness, casting him in the role of the demon lover, a midnight usurper who knows and is the only one to both read and approve the forbidden knowledge behind his truelove's eyes and innocent face. Manfred studies his books on occult knowledge, reading all through the night, greeting the dawn with bleary eyes. The Byronic figure, often a chronic insomniac, desires not only forgetfulness and oblivion but also the rest of sleep, the mind's calming from the cycle of tormenting remorse. The beginning of Manfred shows the pain of impossible sleep.

> The lamp must be replenished, but even then
> It will not burn so long as I must watch:
> My slumbers—if I slumber—are not sleep,
> But a continuance of enduring thought,
> Which then I can resist not. . . . (1.1.1–5)

Manfred's needed sleep and highly strung wakefulness associate him with night journeys, done in lunar light. The stable temporality that flows with the daylight workday and with nighttime sleep is disrupted into a non-working wakefulness. Interrupting the duty of hours, he is outside the workaday world, connected to the evil deeds that happen at night, the guilty pillow, the vampire, and the night-ghoul. Blanchot writes of night as figural for an "outside"—outside the neat circle of the Hegelian dialectic. The circular return of Hegel's thesis/antithesis/synthesis is broken by the secret night of no return, of the journeyer who does not come home.

Byronic lucubration takes on a melancholy hue in Edward Bulwer-Lytton's Newgate novel, *Eugene Aram* (1831). Like the noctambulists Manfred, Faust, and Melmoth, Eugene estranges himself from others by withdrawing into his occult studies. Manfred, Faust, and Melmoth take this research too far—they come to know too much about the supernatural, the superhuman realm, thus becoming too great to dwell with common mortals. Eugene's fugitive retreat from the world comes from both his bloody secret—his role in a man's murder—and his insatiable thirst for knowledge, itself a means of escaping his terrible mindscape. Manfred and his ilk become demonic and otherworldly while Eugene's night studies take him merely into a melancholy darkness. Eugene's guilt, his desire for self-annihilation, lead to the further desire to dissolve his self in knowledge, in his books, in staying up. He holds onto his terror of guilt with a fearful grasp, all the time flinging himself into constant study. "Eugene Aram was a man whose whole life seemed to have been one sacrifice to knowledge" (433). From the beginning of the narrative, Eugene is already cursed with the pangs of remorse, the forsaken sense of an unresting torment. Eugene remarks, "It is a dark epoch in a man's life when sleep forsakes him; when he tosses to and fro, and thought will not be silenced; when the drug and draught are the courters of stupefaction, not sleep; when the down pillow is a knotted log; when the eyelids close but with an effort, and there is a drag, and a weight, and a dizziness in the eyes at morn" (469). Eugene reads to attempt to make time move forward, to avoid the paralysis of his mind caught in his terrible past. The night brings on the phantoms of a lost place in temporality, and even sleep teems with the feverish dreams of the guilty soul. Insomnia needs filling with the eyes moving over pages, the pen scratching the paper.

Sidney Carton in *A Tale of Two Cities* practices self-exiled destruction, a continued search to remain estranged, cast out, and ruined through his feverish night research, fueled by alcohol and despair. Keeping awake while others sleep, Dickens seems to say, undercuts the possibility for Carton to participate in the "honorable ambition, self-denial, and perseverance" that the man of "good abilities and good emotions" (155–56) should uphold. James Eli Adams dubs Carton a "dandy-dilettante" who is an affront to Carlylean earnestness. Carton with "waste forces within him and a desert all around him" is "incapable of his own help and his own happiness, sensible of the blight on him" (155–56). Like the Gothic villain whose blasted life comes from passionate failure, Carton lets his failure "eat him away" and, after a night full of research and reading the law, he "threw himself down in his clothes on a neglected bed, and its pillow was wet with wasted tears" (156). He often stays up nights like this, to help the ambitious Mr. Stryver with his cases. But the benefit of this useful work doesn't fall to Carton; in fact, he uses it as a means to further alienate himself from society by dissipation, which ruins his health. The intensity of his concentration when he lucubrates belies his carelessness in all other parts of his life (except for his desires to sacrifice himself for Lucie) and shows a kind of escape through loss of self-cares (an "anxious gravity" [152]), which is surprising for Carton whose central problems lie in self-absorption. "With knitted brows and intent face, so deep in his task that his eyes did not even follow the hand he stretched out for his glass" (154).

Heathcliff's chronic wakefulness after Catherine's death keeps his nerves highly strung, raking his body such that his nightwalking becomes his only work.[20] Trying to sleep, Heathcliff describes his insomnia, which is caused by Catherine's wandering ghost: "I closed my eyes, she was either outside the window, or sliding back the panels, or entering the room, or even resting her darling head on the same pillow as she did when a child. And I must open my lids to see. And so I opened them a hundred times a-night" (230). Nelly describes him as a person "going blind with loss of sleep" (262). Brontë thus creates Heathcliff as a figure so self-absorbed (and "other"-absorbed, the "other" being Catherine who is, in some sense, still *his* self) that he transcends time and embodiment itself—still in love and haunting the moors after his death. Desire turns inward, feeding on fantasy, auto-obsession, pulling outward the deep interior of the self by wielding it as a weapon of world-decimation, through self-decimation.

While the tortured quality of this starved state is clear, escape also opens as a possibility, pointing to an explanation as to why the outlawry of the Byronic figure is attractive to love narratives. Being either so large that he might trace a line of escape out of the dreary world of common-place concerns, or so slender that he might slip out under cover of the secret night, the Byronic figure traces a path of freedom with his home-lessness. Literally starving oneself, going on a hunger strike might be the only way out of an intolerable existence. When Catherine dies, Heathcliff loses all appetite for things of life in this world, including nourishment of any kind.[21] Byron himself dieted off and on throughout his life, desiring to represent with his body the romantic figure, "pale and slender," as Eisler writes in her popular biography, "haunted by secret sorrow and wasting loss" (120). Being consumed from within, the pallid wraith might become so miniscule he could almost disappear. Slipping away would free him from a dreary life into a fantasy of pure ideals, passion fulfilled.

Even though he represents the ur-hetero-erotic hero, the Byronic hero also, paradoxically, is an exemplary onanist. Eve Sedgwick has done foundational work on the "other" sexuality, onanism, and how it became linked in the early nineteenth century with certain personality traits. She quotes from an 1860 tract on the "masturbating girl" by Augusta Kinsley Gardner, explaining the disabilities of the onanist as one

> in whom the least impression is redoubled like that of a "tam-tam,"
> [yet who seeks] for emotions still more violent and more varied. It
> is this necessity which nothing can appease. . . . It is the emptiness
> of an unquiet and somber soul seeking some activity, which clings

to the slightest incident of life, to elicit from it some emotion which
forever escapes; in short, it is the deception and disgust of existence.
(Quoted in *Tendencies*, 124–25)

The "addiction" to activity that might fill the abyss of the soul but never
does, the repetition of thoughts and the circling restlessness of the tormented mind take us right to the heart of the Byronic erotic. For example,
Childe Harold is "pleasure's palled victim" (1.73.8). He has

> . . . grown agèd in this world of woe,
> In deeds, not years, piercing the depths of life,
> So that no wonder waits him—nor below
> Can Love or Sorrow, Fame, Ambition, Strife,
> Cut to his heart again with the keen knife
> Of silent, sharp endurance. (3.5.1–6)

Byronism itself has always been associated with the insatiability of a self
whose depths of desire and passion exceed the bounds of any satisfaction.
Disappointed and sneering at a society he finds worthless yet still looking,
without even hope of success, for his sweeping ideals, lost somewhere
along the way, the Byronic figure is left only with himself for pleasure and
pain, for a solipsistic erotic repetition. Childe Harold expresses his autoerotic subjectivity: "I *have* thought /Too long and darkly, till my brain
become, / In its own eddy boiling and o'er-wrought / A whirling gulf of
phantasy and flame: / And thus, untaught in youth my heart to tame . . ."
(3.7.1–5). The fascination of Byronism revolves around the nonproductive
economy of the autoerotic, ceaselessly turning inward and hence not
bound by the duties and proprieties of society, of a proscribed "mature,"
heterosexual economy. A "dutiful" eroticism is one that can be circumscribed, traced, understood by its placement among societal duties. But a
restless autoeroticism, not appearing to need the validation or definition of
the other, defines a reckless individualism or sublime subjectivity. And we
must pay particular attention to the sublime here: Byron's heroes, Rochester,
and Heathcliff were created using materials taken from the concept of the
Romantic sublime. Their sublime subjectivity serves as a tool to distinguish
them from many other antiheroic lovers of the nineteenth century. Full of
chaos, the Romantic sublime self spills over in excess. Such a self, like the
Wordsworthian consciousness, could dissolve at any moment into nature,
into unity with the world, or into the black abyss of hell and hence be
utterly lost to representation. The "heights of the soul," as Nietzsche calls
the sublime, reveal the incomprehensibility of an interiority that can
become limitless. The key to sublime subjectivity, as Jean-Luc Nancy

argues in *Of the Sublime: Presence in Question,* lies in its quality of signifying nothing, of being unnameable and uncontainable. As part of this sublime subjectivity, the eroticism of Romantic dangerous lovers mesmerizes
by a profound nescience because one can never fully know the infinite. In
The Romantic Sublime, Thomas Weiskel, refashioning the Kantian sublime to bring it into a psychoanalytic discourse, argues that the sublime is
the self's internalization of the "unattainability of the object," and thus the
ungraspable becomes located within. The lover's sublime works as a meas-
ure of failure—to return to the recurring theme of this project—but at the
same time holds a promise, a freedom, "a movement of being carried away,
traversal, uplifting, transport" (*Sublime,* 7–8) for the hero himself and also
for his lover.[22] Infinite longing marks the divinity of the superior imagination, according to Romantic paradigms, and only those who strive for the
impossible can reach this type of noble failure. Along with this failure
comes the unplumbable depth of the loss of the ability to know oneself or
the other, and this rupture in epistemology defines the sublimity of the
Romantic antihero.

The anatomy of the Byronic erotic sublime often includes a rebellious
doubling of the self in an incestuous self-love.[23] Manfred's love for Astarte
is narcissistic; he states that they had "one heart." Astarte in many ways is
Manfred's erotic externalized, an erotic based on loving, pleasuring the
mirror self. Byron himself found his deepest erotic expression in his incestuous affair with his half sister Augusta, an eroticism of the other as same
as the self, of two creating a completion when brought together.
Autoeroticism has a hidden quality; it hollows out an obscure interiority.
Childe Harold is described:

> Yet oft-times in his maddest mirthful mood
> Strange pangs would flash along Childe Harold's brow,
> As if the Memory of some deadly feud
> Or disappointed passion lurked below:
> But this none knew, nor haply cared to know;
> For his was not that open, artless soul
> That fuels relief by bidding sorrow flow,
> Nor sought he friend to counsel or condole. (1.8.1–8)

As Elfenbein points out, subjectivity cannot be represented because of the
self's secret infinity, yet, in one of the Byronic hero's many contradictions,
because the self is nonrepresentational and must live pleasures and pains
solitarily, it must be witnessed because its nonrepresentability guarantees
its existence. Hence the emphasis in Byronism on confession, expression,
performance, the exhibition of emotions, and the "within" as erotic, yet

also the importance to this paradigm of showing only enough to make it clear how hidden and inaccessible is this soul. [24] The onanist's veiled eroticism, appearing to be self-sufficient in its profundity, defines a self that, like the Byronic Heathcliff, "is so eternally secluded in itself" (320), yet depends on fantasy, confession, witnessing.

The onanist's power lies in the Byronic belief in the possibility of the lone subject making or breaking meaning itself in the world. Power is seated in the self's secret infinity that can turn away from the world yet have it at the same time. The Byronic hero draws the reader, and the romantic heroine, into the untouchability and the unknowability of his mind, with its access into an abyss of blackened meaning, which is somehow, in an uncanny turn, representative of experience itself and hence easily identifiable for his reader. Byron's representations of subjectivity were felt by early nineteenth-century readers, Elfenbein explains, to display so transparently emotional experience that they seemed to be "transcripts" of this experience. The readers and consumers of Byron felt somehow inside the text, as if their experience was the text. This construction could serve as the definition of desire itself: wanting that which eternally withdraws just out of reach, yet which seems somehow to define the desirer herself and all she desires to be. Compelled by the magnetism of interiority, the one outside looks into the veiled and unknown interior, eternally secluded, yet can step in and be, herself, the autoerotic center. Reading can itself also take on this structure, as the nineteenth-century readers of Byron attest. Defining a reading site is a way of describing interiority itself; the space of reading and its interior allegorize the text as interior and then, finally, the interiority of the subject herself.[25] This play of inside/outside points to the simple onanistic eroticism of reading and the way it draws an enchanted circle around the subject and the reading space, magic in its self-contained, self-pleasuring "within-ness."[26] Proust, as a theorist of the act of reading, describes the hiddenness of reading pleasures, the way it creates a "hiding-hole," where he can feel invisible yet observe what occurs on the "outside" of his reading space. [27] Reversing the common paradigms of reading as an act of incorporation and appropriation, Proust argues that, in addition to gathering the read words and their narrative into our minds, and "adding" them to ourselves, as one might add more ingredients to a dish, we also actually live our "exterior" lives, outside the text, *in* the act of reading. Not only this, but many of our memories, our past itself, can be recovered only through opening a book, as if our experience is contained between the two covers. The seductiveness of reading lies in the paradox that sitting with oneself with a book becomes an illusion of empowerment, of the self becoming other, of interiority expanded without bounds, and, at the same time, situated within a book. This model for reading, or allegory for the convolutions of the boundaries of selfhood, also describes the earlier artic- ulation of sublime subjectivity made accessible with the Byronic figure. The Byronic hero is a reader: he creates an erotic out of a desire for the self's infinity, just as all readers do. One of his appeals is as a brooder whose multichambered mind full of layered thoughts is complex enough to always leave food for more brooding.

The lone world of fantasy and the untraceable pleasures of the vast interiority of reading and autoeroticism open possibilities of a sublime escape. Byron himself was fascinated with the act and site of reading and study, especially when forbidden, secretive, and nocturnal. Greedy in his solitary consumption, he made lists of the books he had read before he was ten years old, and his letters are full of references to his reading.[28]

The Byronic figure and even Byron himself, whose celebrity and mythical status made him, to the popular imagination, almost indistinguishable from his created characters, was appropriated, repeated, and plagiarized again and again during his lifetime and after his death.[29] People who knew Byron wrote intimate accounts about him, biographies, or included his conversation in their memoirs. Annabella Millbanke, later Lady Byron, coined the word "Byromania," and she observed that "the Byronic 'look' was mimicked everywhere by people who 'practised at the glass, in the hope of catching the curl of the upper lip, and the scowl of the brow'" (quoted in *Byromania*). What Matthew Arnold described later as the "the-atrical Byron" was also copied by various young dandies by means of "deranging their hair or of knotting their neck handkerchief or of leaving their shirt collar unbuttoned" (*Byromania*, 5). Lady Caroline Lamb, whose affair with Byron was infamous for its drama, extremes, and its develop- ment in a public arena, wrote her fictionalized version of their dangerous love, *Glenarvon* (1816). In this histrionic antiromance, Glenarvon, the Byronic villain, is a ruined genius who feels too much and must steel his heart, setting his sights on ruining others as he has done to himself. He is described: "Yet it was the calm of hopeless despair, when passion, too vio- lent to show itself by common means, concentrates itself at once around the heart, and steels it against every sentiment of mercy" (142). *Glenarvon* recounts how the dangerous lover destroys women's lives; it sees Byron as a vampire who, through his incredible magnetism, attracts women only to suck out their strength by stealing their hearts. Glenarvon warns the hero- ine, "My love is death" (229). The drive in the dangerous lover that makes him dangerous—revenge—takes the blackened heart and turns it into outward violence. Full of vengeance, the dangerous lover wants to assuage his pained existence through making others feel torment as he does. The latent violence in his eyes turns on the whole world a hate that desires destruction. Because the dangerous lover believes everything is fragments of his own mindscape, his self-loathing remorse is a small step away from lashing out at others; his self-punishment so easily becomes other-punishment. Vengeance makes of the past an open present; the present pertains only to the past of pained events that must be requited. The past pains must be relived presently but in a reversed way, with the punisher becoming the punished. The dangerous lover obsesses about this revisitation, reliving, and he desires so strongly to make his violent thoughts reality that all his actions move toward this outcome. The heroine herself stands as a figure for vengeance, and the dangerous lover believes that all avenging might be satiated if he can punish her sufficiently. But in the romantic appropriation of the dangerous lover, and this can be clearly seen in the Brontës, love acts as an interruption, disseminating the hard direction of his thought into a soft generosity toward her redemptive figure; his vengeance turns into a violent love, a passionate embrace. This love is the flip side of revenge, its other being. Love's violence bespeaks hatred transformed.

The Byronic hero, pre-Brontës, attempted, unceasingly, to find a transcendental home in the beloved. Always failing to make this love work, he fell into activities that perpetuated and deepened the state of longing: study and reading, insomnia, anorexia, onanism. The erotics of homesickness as articulated by the Byronic hero shape a concept of subjectivity based on failure—the failure of love, of finding a home, of finding meaning. The homesick subject, always pining, points to an ideal he can never have. But at the heart of this failure lies an ontology of escape, an escape that, out of this very lostness, might complete being. But completion only truly comes post-Byron, with the dangerous lover's place in the midst of love's plenitude.

CHAPTER FOUR

The Absurdity of the Sublime

The Regency Dandy and the
Malevolent Seducer (1825–1897)

I. The Regency Dandy

It is strange but true that woven into the fabric of the contemporary out-cast lover is the very different figure of the nineteenth-century dandy. The dandy's languid excess, his love of exquisite frivolity, his need to be inside the fashionable social circle show a sharp contrast with the starved energy of Byronism. Yet the essential being of both figures can be located in the act of renouncing. The gesture of renunciation is a turning away that always remains in some relationship to what has been spurned: it is a giving up in the midst of an interminable yearning. The Byronic figure dwells in the center of this longing, the dandy takes his desires and materializes them; he turns them into a glittering play of objects, a swirling sense of the world as luxurious surface. The mask suffices, at least temporarily, for both figures; they must hide their need for the renounced behind a gloomy majesty or the perfect cut of a suit.

The dandy's powers came most clearly into play in the Silver-Fork novel. Depictions of glittering high society, the Silver-Forks were also called "fashionable novels" or productions of the "dandy school." Spanning roughly 1825 to 1850, Silver-Forks were set during the Regency period and depicted this time as, famously, full of moral vacuity, dissipation, degeneration. To give a sense of the requirements for the genre, Matthew Whiting Rosa describes the Silver-Fork *Granby:*

> There are sumptuous balls, spirited house parties, excited gambling scenes, heightened by gossipy conversation everywhere—at the breakfast table, at the morning embroidery session, at tea, at the dinner table, and in the drawing room. There is ridicule of the mid-dle classes, an intellectual dandy with enough wit to give him edge, and a beautiful heroine less insipid than usual; there are social

climbers, clever but homely daughters who despise men, and, most indispensable of all, there is Almacks. (71)

A clear historical trajectory of appropriation can be traced here: as Elfenbein argues in his essay "Silver-Fork Byron and Regency England," writers of this formula, especially Benjamin Disraeli, Bulwer-Lytton, and Catherine Gore, appropriate some aspects of Byronism in their aristocratic dandies, especially the cynical, world-weary sophisticate of *Don Juan*. To move this trajectory forward to the twentieth century: the contemporary regency romance culls its fashionable and dissipated rake, ultimately reformed by love, from the Silver-Fork. As mentioned in chapter 1, dandiacal dangerous lovers are common in the twentieth-century historical romance, but the regency romance in particular captures the coxcomb and wit of the nineteenth century and places him in the context of redemption through love. Yet unlike most Silver-Forks, regencies show the rake's reformation; the scapegrace becomes a responsible member of his world again when he meets an unsophisticated girl from outside the margins of his glittering circle. She revivifies his interest in life and the responsibilities of the daily round. Regencies take up the dandy after his fashionable life has "ruined" him, after he has come to realize that his life up till the heroine's entrance has been meaningless.[1] Interestingly, Elfenbein's argument about the Silver-Fork novels he discusses follows a didactic model; the message of the Silver-Fork is that Regency fashionable society is amoral and flawed and must be renounced for a middle-class model of domesticity. While this is certainly not true of the majority of Silver-Forks, the most important ones do typify an often desultory and confused didactic bildungsroman. But the reform of the Silver-Fork dandy happens through politics (Pelham) or an emotional downfall (Vivian Grey) and not through romantic love.[2]

Very different from the Romantic self, which always presents itself at the limit, many early and slightly pre-Victorian representations of the dangerous lover have a relation to sublime interiority characterized by being more conscious of surfaces than depths. The Silver-Fork novel hero exemplifies a move from the hero whose meaning lies in an interior abyss to one who *means* by social performance and who always attains the object of his desire. The dandy is obsessively attentive to fashionable dress, creating an inimitable style that everyone, of course, tries to imitate, and which often develops into outrageous foppishness. His central interests in life lie in his wit; his ability to manipulate and lead a transparent fashionable world; his creation of an exclusive, secret society of *ton*.[3] As Ellen Moers points out in *The Dandy: Brummell to Beerbohm,* control stands as a central concern for the dandy—control of his own appearance, of his manners, of fashions, and of the people around him. The Romantic sublime self's dissolution and quality of always spilling over express deep desires to control and an ultimate frustration (e.g., Heathcliff, Rochester, and Byron's Corsair). The dandy's unique ability to obtain all that he desires, or at least to appear to, and to be the object of desire often creates a cynical end of desire. Ultimate control might lead to a final deadening of all the life that relies on chance, accident, and unpredictability—one of the regency romance dandy's difficulties. Like the narrator of *Don Juan,* the tone of the Silver-Fork holds the superficialities of fashionable life up to a satirical light, seeing through the pettiness of all human endeavors. The cynical, worldly voice easily reads humanity's greed for fame, beauty, and fortune.

Unlike the self-exile of the Byronic hero—the man who fails to live in the everyday world of people—the Silver-Fork dandy is eminently successful as a social animal; he lives and moves as a defining element of what it means to be *inside.* The dandy, unlike the Romantic antihero, lives to represent, to present; he is a play of surfaces, of image, of an aesthetic subjectivity. In Bulwer-Lytton's *Pelham* (1828), the title character decides to "set up a *character.* . . . I thought nothing appeared more likely to be obnoxious to men, and therefore pleasing to women, than an egregious coxcomb: accordingly, I arranged my hair into ringlets, dressed myself with singular plainness and simplicity (a low person, by the by, would have done just the contrary), and, putting on an air of exceeding languor, made my maiden appearance" (25). A dandy's role required, as Domna Stanton points out, the epicure's "divination of the trivial" (39). Hence the dandy's only spirituality lies in an ultrarefined relation to the material object, specifically here personal appearance (the cut of his clothes), food, and horses. The character Russelton in *Pelham,* said to be modeled after Beau Brummell, finds at a young age that he cannot write poetry, so he instead becomes a poet of appearance. "Finding, therefore, that my *forte* was not in the Pierian line, I redoubled my attention to my dress; I *coated* and *cravatted* with all the attention the very inspiration of my rhymes seemed to advise" (73). The text to be deciphered is not a bottomless interior, as with the Romantic hero, but rather the most superficial drapery. That most social of acquirements—manners—are also seen as a site of transcendence. "What a rare gift, by and by, is that of manner! how difficult to define—how much more difficult to impart! Better for a man to possess them, than wealth, beauty, or even talent, if it fall short of genius—they will more than supply all" (31). Pelham "almost die[s] with rapture" (49) over a foie gras. Taste takes precedence over emotional experience: a bad dinner is "*the* most serious calamity . . . for it carries with it no consolation: a buried friend may be replaced—a lost mistress renewed—a slandered character be recovered—even a broken constitution restored; but a dinner, once lost, is irremediable; that day is forever departed; an appetite once thrown away can never, till the cruel prolixity of the gastric agents is over, be regained" (123). With a vast emptiness inside him that can never be filled, the Byronic hero is the figure of insatiable hunger. The dandy satisfies himself by filling himself up in a very un-Romantic way: by eating. While Pelham goes into raptures about the culinary arts, he initially casts a satirical eye on romantic passion. He comments on an acquaintance, "I hear he is since married. He did not deserve so heavy a calamity!" (27). Mr. Trebeck in Thomas Henry Lister's *Granby* (1826) (an early Silver-Fork with its heels still in the eighteenth-century novel of manners—e.g., Maria Edgeworth and Fanny Burney) was also modeled after Beau Brummell. Trebeck "wished to astound, even if he did not amuse; and he had rather say a silly thing than a common-place one" (54). William Hazlett commented that Brummell's sayings "were predicated on devaluing the important through 'utmost nonchalance and indifference' on the one hand, and on the other, on 'exaggerating the merest trifles into matters of importance'" (quoted in Stanton, 43). The dandy's unattainability lies not in a deep interior—a blighted spirit—but rather in superficial externalities such as his genius for inimitable style, a brilliant social intercourse so dazzling it can't be grasped, a performance of personality that is unreadable not because of its obscure hiddenness but rather its oversignification in the realm of the marketplace. It appears sometimes that the dandy's soul can be located by discovering the name of his tailor, his florist, and his horse dealer. Emotions, even subjectivity, take on an inauthenticity and so clearly mirror fashionable desire outside him that the Byronic idea of the utter singularity of the soul is dissolved out into the social world. According to Bulwer-Lytton's son, he intended Pelham as "a person who took to himself the form and color of the society in which he moved" (quoted in Christensen, 46). The sublimity of the dandy takes on a humorous banality; it is the "heights of the soul *from which even tragedy ceases to look tragic*" (my emphasis; 42)—the other half of Nietzsche's words, quoted in the last chapter.

Interestingly, the dandy's influence on the social world was more complicated and far-reaching than as merely the first word of fashion. Bulwer-Lytton was obsessed with Byronism and dandyism in his own personality and dress, as well as in his fiction.[4] Yet he often argued vehemently against the Byronic stance; in the beginning of his career he made a call for reform: "The aristocratic gloom, the lordly misanthropy, that Byron represented, have perished amid the action, the vividness, the life of these times" (quoted in Christensen, 7). He even argues that his Pelham "put[s] an end to Byron's Satanic mania" (quoted in King and Engel, 278). Clearly, his stated project with Pelham is to empty the Byronic hero of his sublime meaning, but this evacuation points again and again to Byronism itself.[5] The dandy's relation to the sublime lies in his opposing it, his consistent gesturing to its outside. Many Silver-Fork heroes define themselves precisely in distinction to the Byronic pose. At the end of *Pelham,* the title character apologizes for not being Werther-like: "forgive me if I have not wept over a "*blighted spirit*" . . . and allow that a man who, in these days of alternate Werters [*sic*] and Worthies, is neither the one nor the other, is, at least, a novelty in print, though, I fear, common enough in life" (230). The depiction of the dandy was a way to domesticate the Byronic figure, to bring him from the outside to the inside; to control him by making the immaterial material.

However, Moers points to characteristics of the dandy that might begin to explain his appropriation by the romance, and they also provide a key to his eroticism. She discusses the subversive aspects of dandyism—the irony of Brummell's status as the perfect gentleman. "The dandy," Moers asserts, "stands on an isolated pedestal of self" (171). Albert Camus felt the dandy stood for the individual in revolt against society: he places himself inside, even as the creator of the inside, yet he uses this inside to foreground his superiority, the elevation that locates him both above and as other. Trebeck in Lister's *Granby* expresses the isolation of misanthropy— thus serving to bring the dandy more clearly into the trajectory of the dangerous lover—by his insolent disdain of earnestness, of real work and caring in the world. "Gracefully indolent," he had a "reputation of being able to do a great deal if he would but condescend to set about it" (52). As Caroline, Trebeck's love interest, thinks to herself, "There was a heartlessness in his character, a spirit of gay misanthropy, a cynical, depreciating view of society, an absence of high-minded generous sentiment, a treacherous versatility, and deep powers of deceit" (77). Trebeck's brilliance, his superior sparkle, tends to be not of this world; his misanthropy ruins him for feeling deep passion for others, for showing any real concern for a society he rules by its superciliousness. His cynical life represents exactly the kind of man who has run through his successes too quickly; like Childe Harold he has "felt the fullness of satiety . . ." (I, 34) and he is "secure in guarded coldness . . . and deem'd his spirit now so firmly fixed" that it is "sheath'd with an invulnerable mind" (3.82–85). While seeming somehow "used up" by depleting the sources and life of the world, Trebeck might also, like the Byronic figure, have an interior void, where the endless riches of life and love he obtains instantly drain away.

Another particularly Victorian translation of the Romantic dangerous lover with a mix of Byronic sublimity and early nineteenth-century antiheroic epicurism can be found in Disraeli. Disraeli's Silver-Fork dandy, in *Vivian Grey* (1826), moves from being a Pelham-like star to a self full of a melancholy sublimity, tempered from the wild passions of Byron and the

Gothic and softened from tragedy to a pallid sadness. Vivian Grey exemplifies what could be called a "hinged" sublime. The "hinge" refers to the way the Silver-Fork dandy throws out nonmeaning here and there but will sometimes, suddenly, point to a secret interiority of meaning. And this hinge turns on failure; when the brilliantly successful dandy begins to fail, he moves toward sublimity, as well as the kind of Byronism that later dangerous lovers exemplify. Vivian Grey's astonishingly influential personal charm and his genius for literary quotation and wit bring him, at a young age, to the center of the *haute ton*.[6] Vivian is a dandy of the intellectual type, as opposed to the picturesque kind: here we can mark the contrast of the hidden soul in its brilliancy and infinity—the intellectual dandy—to the glittery externality of the soul—the apparent or picturesque dandy. Vivian, while a dandy, is far more ambitious than the typical picturesque type; he "was a graceful, lively lad, with just enough of dandyism to preserve him from committing gaucheries, and with a devil of a tongue" (17). His constant study is of human nature, how to please and win over others. The intellectual dandy often hides behind his bright, frivolous façade the activity of the researcher who studies both books and the ways of men.[7] Pelham admits that "there has not been a day in which I have spent less than six hours reading and writing" (201).[8] He also often hides the ambitious politician, and, sometimes, the romantic soul which feels deeply. As Matthew Whiting Rosa argues, the dandy, as a fashionable fop, needs to be a literary man, yet he has to hide his hours and hours of study. Intellectuality, like every other accomplishment, needs to appear effortless for the illustrious young buck. Hence a secret interior, a Byronic private soul, distinguishes the intellectual dandy, a superior man among men.

In his bid for a place in Parliament, Vivian Grey wheedles his way into the good graces of several influential politicians only to find, when his prize seems within reach, his "friends" turning against him for petty and backbiting reasons. Forced to fight a duel, he accidentally kills a man whom he deeply esteems. Vivian weeps "as men can weep but once in this world" and flees the country, disaffected with society, bitter with his life and his own false and manipulative ways. "He felt himself a broken-hearted man, and looked for death, whose delay was no blessing" (175). Vivian Gray appears here as a tempered Byronic hero, a softened Manfred. Vivian Grey's fallenness doesn't lead him to exile, or to transcendental homelessness and all the world-hating bitterness that a Manfredian Byronic hero would feel. Manfred and his ilk become demonic and otherworldly, while Vivian Grey's torments take him merely into a melancholy darkness.[9] The melancholy sublime, as Weiskel argues, differs from what could be called a powerful, satanic one because, in the latter, the realization of the self's abyss, of the terror of annihilation and harm, leads to an aggressive identification with what terrorizes, what causes failure. This type of identification brings with it various forms of grandly destructive impulses, to a laying waste on a large scale. Mournful sublimity lacks the grandeur of Manfred and the malevolence of Melmoth or Heathcliff. The melancholy sublime comes from another kind of identification with this aggressive instinct, one that causes feelings of defeatist guilt, partially or wholly sublimated, which brings about a gloomy, thoughtful sense of loss. The Romantics' freedom to delve into transcendence, leading to a positive, Wordsworthian sublime, or a negative Byronic one, shifts here to a wearied worrying, a feeling of agitation and oppression.

Vivian Grey finds himself desired by the *ton* in Europe for very Byronic reasons; he represents now a gloomy mysterious figure. He retains his ability to please fashionables, to be an astute satirical eye on the empty manners of the upper classes. A disappointed man, he is not exactly a ruined one. His world is not Byronically blackened; rather, it is painted in subtle tints of blue. Melancholy evacuates the present of immanent meaning, leaving only a pale semblance of life, an empty play of glittering movement. Gently lost, not angry, Vivian Grey falls in love with a woman who might be his salvation, but he is doubly cursed when she dies suddenly of consumption. In the end, Vivian disappears in an apocalyptic storm, not as a part of its own elemental power—as Manfred would feel—but rather as another stroke of bad luck, a closing stroke in a promising life which ends in failure. Vivian Grey, unlike Manfred or the Corsair, sees his failure as stemming from a lack within him, a failure to see deeply enough, to understand fully, to make a positive decision at the right time. Hamlet-like, Vivian Grey is sad for the whole world; he mourns it, caresses it with his lamentation. Like a young Werther, he falls into the *Heiligtum des Schmerzes,* the worship of sorrow.

In addition to heroes who fail and are overcome by melancholy or a cynical recklessness or weariness, another trait of both the Silver-Fork novel and the contemporary regency romance is the satirizing of certain aspects of the Byronic pose. Byron in some sense preempted such a stance by himself ridiculing the Byronic pose in *Don Juan.* We have already seen some of this deliberate un-Byronizing in *Pelham,* and its manifestation in the Victorian period takes on a moral taint. Thackeray and Carlyle, representing a Victorian disapproval of the wasteful, selfish, and idle type, famously criticize what they see as the silliness and final immorality of the dandy and the particularly Byronic aspects of the dandy.[10] Rosa argues that Silver-Forks culminate in *Vanity Fair* (1848). Thackeray here does even more explicitly what many Silver-Forks have already done: criticize the moral vacuity of Regency society and particularly of the Regency dandy.[11]

Jos Sedley represents the puffed-out, indolent, false self, a heap of clothes who can only repeat again and again a few simple stories about himself that have little basis in fact. His only success lies in his resplendent personal appearance: "A very stout, puffy man, in buckskins and Hessian boots, with several immense neckclothes, that rose almost to his nose, with a red striped waistcoat and an apple-green coat with steel buttons almost as large as crown pieces (it was the morning costume of a dandy or blood of those days)" (29). A picturesque dandy, he revels like Pelham in food and drink, yet unlike Pelham he represents merely an empty joke, an attempted gesture at a once successful performance which now only tries to shore up usefulness, waste, the dead end of everyone's scorn. George Osborne, while something of a dandy, puts on a performance of erotic Byronism. "George had an air at once swaggering and melancholy, languid and fierce. He looked like a man who had passions, secrets, and private harrowing griefs and adventures. His voice was rich and deep. He would say it was a warm evening, or ask his partner to take an ice, with a tone as sad and confidential as if he were breaking her mother's death to her, or preluding a declaration of love" (202). Yet Thackeray's continual deflation of George as not worthy of Amelia's love, as a superfluous being whose selfishness wounds others, serves to point to Byronism as merely a gesture, since George is never any of these things; he's only a selfish cad.

But with the true dandy, there always remains some quality about him that can not be fully explicated. Like the dangerous lover, the dandy's mythic stature, his symbolic stance of always pointing to something larger and indefinable, create a character that is both complete and difficult to permeate. His wholeness of meaning (or meaninglessness) and his success belie dissection, linearity, teleology. Moers writes similarly of the mesmerism of the dandy, represented by Beau Brummell. "There remains an indescribable firmness to the Brummell figure, something compounded of assurance, self-sufficiency, misanthropy, nastiness, even cruelty that made him feared in his lifetime and will never be explained away" (38). The "firmness" or complexity of the dandy character frees him to represent a plethora of identity traits, contradictory posturings, and moral messages. His flatness can be spread out to signify almost endlessly, and from this comes the difficulty in describing definitively his relationship to Byronism and the dangerous lover.

II. The Malevolent Seducer

Always existing as a possibility for the dangerous lover is a fall into the deeps of pure evil. Complete embitterment leaves no moral sense; it leads to rampant, glowing vengeance on the innocent as well as the guilty. All dangerous lovers must be on the fragile edge of this abyss in order to be truly dangerous. Many Gothic villains exist on this plane as do a particularly Victorian translation of the dangerous lover that connects him to an Iago tradition of purposeless malignity. A force for meaningless evil, for destroying the possibility of grace for others, for general, wholesale harm, Iago characters do not even have the excuse of psychologized misanthropy. Their evil participates in a paucity of unique signification; it comes out of some impersonal force of destruction that resides outside reasoning and sense. Often, as in *Othello,* such absurdity of malevolence causes a concatenation of death and destruction; evil spins out of control, affecting a whole scene and all those characters within it. Iago characters open a wound in the world which, in the paradigm of the contemporary romance, is "healed" by the heroine's love. The evil seducer fascinated the mid-nineteenth-century popular imagination in seduction narratives in the penny magazines of the 1840s and 1850s. Sally Mitchell describes the repetition of these narratives in magazines such as the *Pioneer:* the story would include an aristocrat who would seduce a lower-class girl, usually ruin her, then disappear, or be punished by remorse. Clearly a class allegory and certainly a reaction against Byronism, these narratives represent the dangerous lover not as an unquiet soul searching for absolution or death, but rather as *only* dangerous (but still titillating in his dangerousness). Mitchell also points to numerous sensation novels that contain seduction narratives, such as A. J. Barrowcliffe's *Normanton* (1862), *The Soiled Dove, Jessie's Expiation* (1867), and James Malcolm Rymer's *The White Slave* (1844–45).[12] Iago-like antiheroes often serve, for the Victorians, as transgressors of the social norm, whose punishment leads to a reaffirmation of normative reason. Ellen Wood, in *East Lynne* (1861), creates the heartless rake Frank Levison who vilifies the dandy.[13] Unlike the most successful dandies of the Regency, Levison vulgarly overdresses. Not only does he have "perfumed hands" and "dainty gloves," but "He would wear diamond shirt-studs, diamond rings, diamond pins; brilliants, all of first water" (97). Like the dandies of the Silver-Forks, he runs into debt living a high and frivolous life, and he also tries out politics. Yet in many ways he is unsuccessful as a dandy; while he seduces many women, he finally becomes merely a source of harm for those around him. His seduction of Lady Isabel (Mrs. Carlyle) points to the didactic thread of the novel; such idle, wasteful, and cruel men are harmful to society as a whole. Motivated by no purpose, Levison seduces various women; he divides families and even commits murder. He does these things without any sort of magnetism, personal power, or clear desire. As a purely transgressive force, he still does not create a serious rift or interruption in given norms, as a rebellious Romantic would seek to do, but rather serves only to uphold the generally understood moral structure based on heterosexual marriage and monogamy. While we might bring this antihero into a Sadean discourse, in this sense he is not Sadean. Sade seeks to outrage, as Pierre Klowossowski asserts, and to outrage is, among other things, to establish a site of singularity in the midst of the general geography of society, a unique stance in the center of universal reason. "With this principle of the normative generality of the human race in mind, Sade sets out to establish a countergenerality that would obtain for the specificity of perversions, making exchange between singular cases of perversion possible" (Klowossowski, 14). The Victorian antihero, on the contrary, can always be recuperated into a heterosexual discourse of crime and punishment. He may stand out starkly in his dangerous eroticism initially, but as the novel draws to a close, he is punished, chastened, and somehow brought under the shadow of propriety.

Following the bifurcated erotic structure of many Victorian novels, *East Lynne* centers on the two-lover motif. The heroine has two possible erotic outlets; she is drawn in two directions and she is forced to choose: one lover represents the propriety of the secure gentleman situated in steady society (Mr. Carlyle) and the other the abyssal secretiveness of the lost stranger, generally utterly villainous (Levison). To some extent reminiscent of the relationship of the Gothic heroine to the villain and her lover as discussed in chapter 2, this paradigm usually posits, similarly and not surprisingly, the villain as the more deeply fascinating and sexually attractive of the two for the heroine. We have only to think of Linton and Heathcliff in *Wuthering Heights* for a classic study of the confusion of this duality for the heroine and its possibility for tragically pulling her into unlivable fragments. Anne Humpherys theorizes about the way the Victorian gothic has taken up and rearranged the Gothic villain, using some pieces in one prototypical character, and others in a different one. In the early Victorian gothic, one type of villain, as Humpherys explains, is created as a kind of Byronic hero who doesn't commit a deep crime or sin but still feels a misanthropic guilt and melancholy (like the later Vivian Grey, Rochester, and the many less dangerous contemporary romance dangerous lovers, especially in the "sweet" genres), and the other acts in villainous ways yet doesn't contain the psychological depth of the Gothic villain. This second type—which Humpherys calls the melodramatic villain—generally acts the part of the villain in the Victorian two-lover motif, although the variations of this character abound. Steerforth in Dickens's *David Copperfield* (1846) can be classed as just such a rootless and depthless evil-doer: why does he do it? We never really know.

Steerforth begins by condescending to David when they are children at Salem House, and such a domineering and dictatorial manner, with his upper-class appearance of experience and knowledge, immediately charms the slavishly passive and class-obsessed David. David precipitously falls in love, and their homoerotic relationship blinds David to Steerforth's savage sadism—generally worked against those of lower classes, such as the schoolteacher Mr. Mell whom Steerforth torments because his mother lives on charity in an almshouse. Yet Steerforth holds this charm, the charm of cultural capital, which creates the self-ease and assurance David always wishes he had. "There was an ease in his manners—a gay and light manner it was, but not swaggering—which I still believe to have borne a kind of enchantment with it. I still believe him, in virtue of his carriage, his animal spirits, his delightful voice, his handsome face and figure, and, for aught I know, of some inborn power of attraction besides (which I think a few people possess), to have carried a spell with him to which it was a natural weakness to yield, and which not many persons could withstand" (124–25). The entrancing nature of the dangerous lover comes from his power and the desire for immolation at the feet of the beautiful God who demands prostration. Steerforth enchants numerous people in this manner, most fatally Emily. Emily could choose the simple, honest, working-class Ham (and even David appears as a possibility for a time), but she instead falls under the spell of the "demon lover"—the impossible, devilishly eroticized Steerforth. Unlike the pure Byronic hero who is fallen and survives as a failure, a character like Dickens's Steerforth once fallen must die to the narrative, be effaced by it rather than transcend it or hold its immanent meaning. In Dickens's story of two lovers, both flawed, *Dombey and Son* (1847), Edith comes to have a choice between her husband, Mr. Dombey, who stands for the frigidity of an obsession with business and money—his coldness freezes all those around him—or Carker, who can be placed firmly in the Iago tradition. With his melodramatic flair, he is a theatrical, gestural dangerous lover who seems to have no interiority, hiding his abyss behind his large grin and debonair façade. Like many antiheroic lovers, he holds steadily to a mask that controls his emotions and hides the chilling emptiness inside. "He had his face so perfectly under control, that few could say more, in distinct terms, of its expression, than that it smiled or that it pondered" (457). A kind of cat or predatory animal, he "pounces" on his victims and, metaphorically, tears them up. "Coiled up snugly at certain feet, he was ready for a spring, or for a tear, or for a scratch . . ." (387). His divining cleverness and sensitivity to the subtle emotions and desires of others complicates him and explains how he is able both to repulse and to enchant the women in the novel, specifically

Florence, Alice, and Edith. While these women all come to hate Carker, he represents for each of them the beauty of a Sadean mind. Florence's reaction to him, while never that of a lover, expresses strongly his hypnotic qualities:

> This conduct on the part of Mr. Carker, and her habit of often considering it with wonder and uneasiness, began to invest him with an uncomfortable fascination in Florence's thoughts. A more distinct remembrance of his features, voice, and manner: which she sometimes courted, as a means of reducing him to the level of a real personage, capable of exerting no greater charm over her than another: did not remove the vague impression. And yet he never frowned, or looked upon her with an air of dislike or animosity, but was always smiling and serene. (385)

Florence's "wonder and uneasiness" has an undeveloped erotic aspect to it; she responds to his mysterious otherness with a kind of queasy desire to be mastered. Similarly, Carker's seduction of Alice appears at first to have made her his worst enemy, but she suddenly relents when it comes to the possibility of Carker's death. Edith's response to Carker initially seems to be merely a proud desire to use him as a tool for revenge: running away with Carker will punish Dombey for his sadistic treatment of her. And Edith punishes Carker as well by only pretending she will become his mistress and then renouncing him when he has become a means for escape. Yet Edith's attraction to him is certainly more subtle and varied, as Humpherys argues convincingly; it is an attraction of similar temperaments, and in their relationship we see Carker as a handsome and sensual man. Carker's erotic villainy places him firmly in the trajectory of the dangerous lover, and yet he does not stand radically outside as a blackened, world-decimating type such as Manfred or Heathcliff. While there are moments when the reader is persuaded to identify with him because he is shown to have an interior life, Carker's evil never holds an erotic sublimity.

When Maggie Tulliver first meets Stephen Guest in Eliot's *The Mill on the Floss* (1860), she sees in him "the half-remote presence of a world of love and beauty and delight, made up of vague, mingled images from all the poetry and romance she had ever read, or had ever woven in her dreamy reveries" (311). Stephen Guest's "diamond ring, attar of roses, and air of nonchalant leisure, at twelve o'clock in the day" and his characterization as "the graceful and odiferous result of the largest oil-mill and the most extensive wharf in St. Ogg's" (193) mark him as the idle dandy, backed by cultural and economic capital. The erotic intensity Maggie feels

in his presence comes not only from his figure symbolizing an aestheti-
cized and ideal world but also from his very inaccessibility and taboo status as her cousin Lucy's lover. His dangerousness stems from the way he
envelops a lost and thus paradisiacal world for Maggie who is drawn to
him as she is drawn to other self-destructive rebellious passions. We have
seen these desires at play in her childhood, in the scene where she cuts off
her hair or when she runs away to live with the gypsies. "Something
strange and powerful there was in the light of Stephen's long gaze, for it
made Maggie's face turn towards it and look upwards at it" (357). Stephen
Guest's seduction of Maggie comes from his selfish and spoiled misdirec-
tion rather than a deliberate desire for another's harm—the motivating
influence of characters like Carker and Steerforth. Stephen has the ability
to take a position on the margins of the moral world of the novel, as Neil
Roberts suggests; "he is the useless product of other men's labour" (99).[14]
He is certainly a force exterior to Maggie's world, a stranger to her experience up until the moment she meets him; and it is this strangeness that
intoxicates Maggie. When she succumbs to "that strong mysterious charm
which made a last parting from Stephen seem the death of all joy" (379),
Maggie finally closes the book on the possibility of being accepted into the
society of St. Ogg's: she dooms herself to an exiled state, full of sadness,
wasted lives, lost causes.

The Mill on the Floss, not surprisingly, contains the two-lover motif,
but Eliot divides the Byronic hero/villain into two men, equally unfit to
be proper lovers for Maggie. While not exactly a melodramatic villain,
Stephen does become the seducer. Philip Wakem takes the place of the
more proper lover in the lover's triangle because of his deep love for
Maggie and the fact that he is romantically unattached (although because
of their families having quarreled, their relationship is also impossible),
yet he represents the kind of lover Humpherys discusses in her schema.
Because of his hunched back, he feels he has been "marked from childhood for a peculiar kind of suffering" (271). He has a Byronized melancholy torment about him without having committed any crimes, and his
deformed figure marks him as marginalized and Cain-like.[15]

One text we must locate in this history because of the way it weaves
together many of the threads we have been following is Oscar Wilde's *The
Picture of Dorian Gray* (1890). While not exactly a two-lover narrative,
Wilde's novel skillfully combines the Silver-Fork narrative (at its most
didactic) and the seduction narrative. Dorian Gray works as an important
transitional figure in the dangerous lover trajectory; he represents the philosophy of the dandy with his worship of the beautiful, yet he is also a
destructive seducer and rake, driving numerous women and men to ruin
and suicide. As Basil remarks, "Why is your friendship so fatal to young

men? There was that wretched boy in the Guards who committed suicide. . . . There was Sir Henry Ashton, who had to leave England, with a tarnished name. . . . What about Lord Kent's only son, and his career? . . . What about the young Duke of Perth?" (147). Dorian, akin to the vampire, the rake of the seduction narrative, and Gothic villains, ruins lovers in order to feed his desire for all types of tabooed and marginal experiences, to further his attempts to reach the depths of selfish pleasures and abasement. This spiral towards "sin" begins with the dandy's divination of materiality—food, wine, clothing, art.

> Fashion, by which what is really fantastic becomes for a moment universal, and Dandyism, which, in its own way, is an attempt to assert the absolute modernity of beauty, had, of course, their fascination for him. His mode of dressing, and the particular styles that from time to time he affected, had their marked influence on the young exquisites of the Mayfair balls and Pall Mall club windows, who copied him in everything that he did, and tried to reproduce the accidental charm of his graceful, though to him only half-serious, fopperies. (127)

But the "worship of the senses" is not enough for him; he wants to live a new "hedonism" that will explore every kind of passionate experience. The dandy in his purist form shows no true passion; his highest achievement is to be bored with all that is exquisite and sublime. But finally Dorian goes down a very different path from the Silver-Fork dandy: he revels in the corruption, the vacuity at the heart of beauty. Beauty only reaches its highest culmination when it touches death and decay. As an Aesthete, Dorian is also a late Romantic. "There were moments when he looked on evil simply as a mode through which he could realize his conception of the beautiful" (143). Even in Thackeray's critique of the dandy in *Vanity Fair* he is never a force for evil.

Basil Hallward, drawn by the aesthetic experience of gazing on Dorian's still-beautiful person, tells Lord Henry about the kind of seduction Dorian is able to practice. "When our eyes met, I felt that I was growing pale. A curious sensation of terror came over me. I knew that I had come face to face with someone whose mere personality was so fascinating that, if I allowed it to do so, it would absorb my whole nature, my whole soul, my very art itself" (6). The homoeroticism of the narrative points to the way Wilde's representation of the "dangerousness" of our hero comes from society's fear of same-sex desire. Clearly Dorian's evil influence on men and his later punishment by disfiguration and death is shot through with homophobia. The secret expression of his sin, locked away in the attic, has much to do with a figurative meaning of being in "the closet"—forced to hide one's desires and sexual activities. Never redeemed by love as a contemporary romantic antihero would be, Dorian dies, a self exhausted by passionate experience that is never enough to fulfill him. Dorian's Gothic double—a painting which changes to reflect his evil deeds while his own appearance remains youthful and innocent-looking—has Dorian's sins and evil deeds inscribed on its face. Like many other dangerous lovers, such as the Cain-like Byronic figure, Dorian's unspeakable interiority is marked on an exterior surface, the painting. Thus the existence of the unrepresentable relies on a surface inscription, which could be read by anyone. Basil sums up this central truism that drives the plot: "Sin is a thing that writes itself across a man's face. It cannot be concealed. People talk sometimes of secret vices. There are no such things. If a wretched man has a vice, it shows itself in the lines of his mouth, the droop of his eyelids, the moulding of his hands even" (146). Of course, when the inscription is destroyed, the man is destroyed, pointing again to the paradoxical play of surface/depth of the dangerous lover.

III. The Vampire

It seems fitting to end this history with a figure that has been haunting it all along, with a character who himself is also always located *afterward*, after death, after the end of all narrative movement and life. One of the repeated refrains of this project, found both in its overall structure and meaning as well as its theoretical underpinnings, is the narrativity of the "too-late." The drama of the dangerous lover begins when it is already over, after the hero feels his being has no meaning anymore. The story is generated out of this death of ideals, of futurity. Our being itself is defined by a relation with death more so than with origins just as the dangerous lover narrative moves fluidly into and out of a dwelling in death, in fragments, interruptions, failure. The collection of antiheroes who most exemplify this paradoxical afterlife begins with Melmoth, who has sold his soul to the devil and symbolizes all lost and homeless beings such as Cain and the Wandering Jew. Out of Byron's fascination with cursed, unredeemable figures comes the character Manfred, whose story begins with an all-consuming longing for death and ends with his actual death, which pales in meaning when compared to the power of the death-in-life of the beginning of the story. Childe Harold has used up his life in idle dissipations when his story starts, and his journey begins without object or return. *The Giaour* opens on a blackened, sterile life, full only of a desire for vengeance which, once slaked, means death. Lara returns to his homeland after many years of travel in a state of afterlife:

> There was in him a vital scorn of all:
> As if the worst had fall'n which could befall,
> He stood a stranger in this breathing world,
> An erring spirit from another hurled;
> A thing of dark imaginings, that shaped
> By choice the perils he by chance escaped;
> But 'scaped in vain, for in their memory yet
> His mind would half exult and half regret. (1.17.1–8)

This "stranger in this breathing world" mourns the past, mourns life and a place among the living. Heathcliff's origins are always obscured, and his resulting estrangement from the society of the narrative points, from the beginning, to a cursed existence. Rochester enters the story of *Jane Eyre* sneering at the world from his blighted life, feeling everything is lost to him. Max de Winter of *Rebecca* steps into the heroine's life in a state of frozen bitterness. Revivified through the love of the heroine, his afterlife becomes more fully imminent than his life before the beginning of the story.

The figure of the vampire literalizes the undead state of the dangerous lover. The vampire's near immortality links him to Cain, the Wandering Jew, and those ghastly characters in Byron who live eons of pain in a matter of days. In John Polidori's introduction to his *The Vampyre* (1819), he points out that vampirism was often considered as a punishment after death for some dark crime committed when living, and the punishment encompassed not only the torment of a lonely and desolate immortality, but also the compulsion to visit the curse on those most loved by the man when alive. Byron's Giaour is just such a cursed soul:

> But first on earth, as Vampyre sent,
> Thy corse shall from its tomb be rent;
> Then ghastly haunt the native place,
> And suck the blood of all thy race;
> There from thy *daughter, sister, wife,*
> At midnight drain the stream of life;
> *Yet loathe the banquet which perforce*
> Must feed thy livid living corse. (755–62)

The dangerous lover vampirizes those who love him, as with Manfred's driving Astarte to take her own life; Glenarvon's seduction of his victims, which leave them pale and lifeless; and the hero of the modern gothic

romance and the erotic historical whose mysterious and terrifying eroticism fascinates the heroine into a helpless passivity. The Victorian seduction narrative often likens the seducer to a kind of vampire like Dorian
Gray, or a frenzied animal like Carker who might attack with fangs. The
vampire, like the dangerous lover, steps out of timeless myth. In both
myths eroticism might bring about death, transformation, or a transcendence of time and place. Both trace their roots to the Gothic demon who
rises out of a supernatural realm of superior strength, agility, and the ability to change shape and form. Those who were already marginalized figures in society were thought to return as vampires after death, Laurence
Rickels explains. In medieval Eastern Europe alcoholics, thieves, excom-
municated people, non-Christians (specifically Jews), those who died
under a curse, and suicides were some of the excluded who might not stay
dead. Dangerous lovers come down through myth with a similar constellation of vampiric symptoms; they are often alcoholics (Carton, Rhett
Butler, and numerous erotic historical romance heroes), thieves (Conrad,
the Corsair, and many other pirates); they are seen as unholy or cursed
(Manfred, the Gaiour, Cain-like figures, Rochester, Heathcliff, and contemporary heroes linked with demonism, especially in gothic romances);
they are effeminate or gay-coded (Rhett Butler, the dandy); and they
desire death above all else (Manfred, Carton, Heathcliff, etc.). Vampires
after Byron, Tom Holland argues, descend from the Byronic hero, and
Bram Stoker's *Dracula* (1897), surely the most influential version of the
vampire story, was largely based on Polidori's *The Vampyre* (1819), a story
Holland notes was originally told by Byron, which his sometime doctor
heard, recorded, and embellished.[16] Contemporary film versions of vampirism, as well as such popular narratives as those of Anne Rice, represent
an even more eroticized, sophisticated, celebrity vampire haunting the
fashionable world with dandified grace, full of Byronic decadence, satiated ennui, melancholy, and pallid beauty.

   An interesting and tenuous link can be traced between the vampire and
the dandy, with Byronism as a background influence for both. Curiously,
Lord Ruthven of *The Vampyre* appears to be something of a Regency
dandy, and he has many of the characteristics that the Silver-Fork will later
incorporate for its hero. The story opens in a familiar way:

> It happened that in the midst of the dissipations attendant upon a
> London winter, there appeared at the various parties of the leaders
> of the *ton* a nobleman, more remarkable for his singularities, than
> his rank. . . . His peculiarities caused him to be invited to every
> house; all wished to see him, and those who had been accustomed
> to violent excitement, and now felt the weight of ennui, were

pleased at having something in their presence capable of engaging their attention. (265)

Lord Ruthven has "the reputation of a winning tongue," and he loves to gamble, especially when it means he can ruin promising young men, Dorian Gray-like. He moves through the drawing rooms of London with a magnetic aloofness, "a man entirely absorbed in himself, who gave few other signs of his observation of external objects, than the tacit assent to their existence, implied by the avoidance of their contact" (267). He has, like so many dangerous lovers, "the possession of irresistible powers of seduction" (269). Lord Ruthven, like all vampires, is a dangerous lover of the melodramatic villainous type, and he eroticizes a sexual cannibalism, an act that involves violent, sadistic seduction. Because the vampire must always be invited in, he represents the paradoxical fascination and repulsion of sex that is desirable because it is dangerous, because it might lead to pain, expulsion, and/or death. This desire to be ravished, to be "taken," to be greedily consumed, has a role in so many of the demon lover narratives discussed here.

When Jonathan Harker first meets the vampire of Stoker's *Dracula,* his charm and personable qualities relax Harker after his frightful journey. Although when Dracula is later encountered in England he is repeatedly described as a kind of crazed animal with a "hellish" look and flaming red eyes, here in the beginning his gently seductive and thoughtful manners draw Harker to him. Like the many melancholy heroes we have encountered he remarks, "I love the shade and the shadow, and would be alone with my thoughts when I may" (26). Dracula is another night brooder like Manfred or Eugene Aram who must do his work under cover of the darkness, when others are safe within their beds. Cast out of the everyday activities of the living and the permanent stasis of the dead, Dracula haunts the night caught in a liminal state between death and life. Like a melancholy insomniac—Romeo, for instance—he is unable to live in the light of day. Dracula mourns the many who have died during his very long lifetime, both by his hand and by other means. Rickels explains that Dracula represents, like Heathcliff after Catherine's death or Manfred, unmitigated mourning. Dracula apologizes for his melancholia in one of his few speeches: "[M]y heart, through the weary years of mourning over the dead, is not attuned to mirth" (26). Dracula must die in order to open the possibility for a future that comes from Mina's repurification after being "sullied" by Dracula and her engendering of a new narrative through her baby by Harker. That Mina can become a part of the heterosexual couple again and can escape the "outside" as represented by vampirism points to the future of many dangerous lover narratives. Thus we are brought full circle to the collection of dark, mysterious strangers in the twentieth century whose crimes do not need to be expiated by death, or by the punishments and inquietude that might happen after death, but instead their immanence comes on earth and in life, and their terrible self-exiled bitterness is absolved by love in the contemporary romance.

Conclusion

The erotic antihero, so deeply condemned and condemning, arrives in the twentieth century with the weight of the world on his shoulders. Yet for all its darkness, dangerous love might exemplify an escape—from a need for synthesis, from a return to the self and society, from a coming back from the outside. The possibility of transcending time and embodiment through a self- and world-decimation opens up as a possibility for the outcasts. But the escape most apparent and ubiquitous in dangerous lover narratives today is through love. In contemporary romance, we find that the eternal exile, the Cain or forever cursed wanderer, is appropriated into a narrative whose final meaning is grace, revivification, and immanence through love. Love becomes the religion at the end of this itinerary that begins with the Gothic hero, runs through Byronism, the dandy, and the seducer to the contemporary romance. Through a narrative that is constantly failing and dying, love opens up as a transcendent truth which *could* repair the fabric of being, which *might* bring authenticity and presence to the self and the other. The eternal outcast is redeemed in the romance of today. The Gothic villain who could not speak need now only say "I love you" and his torments end in enchantment.

Contemporary romance creates allegories for ontology but it also reaches for answers to the angst-ridden questioning of such theories. Standing just on the edge of the dark abyss, the tragic hero is plucked back just in time by the heroine's pure radiance. The one who falls instead of reaching this final salvation reminds us of types of subjectivity dear to modernists and postmodernists: the one who not only no longer believes, but who has forgotten that faith did once exist. The dangerous lover plays always on this edge, on the edge of the self fragmenting into inarticulateness, into dead ends that might become beginnings. In all of the literary historical threads discussed here we have the subject whose interiority reflects, to varying degrees, the blight of the dark world and its wasteland. In some sense, all the evils of the world are brought to bear on this character—he commits them and they are done to him; he sins and is victimized by the heaviest moral travesties. Melmoth loses his soul to the devil and must move continually to drag other souls into the same hell. The passionate idealism of the Byronic hero, perverted by too much experience too soon, by reaching the limits of knowledge with too great an intellectual power and exhausting the stores of the world too quickly, causes his fall from the grace of transcendence, of immanent meaning. He fights his fate with violence against others, passionate self-destruction, dark dealings with demonism and night hauntings. Closely aligned with death—the death of meaning, the death of being, the death of salvation—this figure mourns the loss of his ideal self, of a meaningful world, of a being that fulfills and can fulfill others. The cursed figure of the dangerous lover begins his narrative after his world has been blighted; his story exists in a spectral afterlife—*after* life has failed, *after* possibility itself has been long gone. His relation to meaning has become secretive, furtive, and any relationship he is able to establish with the other takes on this inarticulate quality, described by secret whispering, speeches that point to obscured meanings on the other side of life.

As we have seen, tracing the erotic outcast through the last two hundred years and through a number of important philosophical paradigms recuperates the romantic figure of the dangerous lover as a nexus of ideas profoundly influential in the way we define subjectivity today. This history also uncovers the much-hidden dialogue that exists between the most difficult and important continental philosophers and the most formulaic of female-coded genres. The literary history delineated here not only links products of an aesthetic based on women's desires and pleasures, but it expresses the need to study these desires as a basis for understanding contemporary constructions of subjectivity. Through the theories of time, being, and selfhood of Heidegger and others we see how the outcast hero and the attraction to him represent ontology itself: the ways our being becomes authentic when it approaches the strange, foreign, and frightening. Although these philosophers do not use love as a theoretical grounding point—in fact, Heidegger in particular is silent on the topic—it is in love narratives that ontology is so clearly explained and understood. In fact, the romance gives us a new perspective on Heidegger's theory of ontology. Out of the Gothic hero and his history we have seen the way the melancholy outcast defines himself as the mourner for the beloved: love equals loss. The Byronic hero describes an early version of modern subjectivity later theorized by Lukács as transcendental homelessness: without any hope of spiritual belonging. Both the dandy's self and that of the evil seducer are empty of meaning, and this evacuation becomes erotic.

Finally, it is really to the Gothic that we must turn in order to understand any dangerous lover figure and his origins. The history of the dangerous lover begins with the Gothic; the enigmatic Gothic villain has yet to become a lover in the stories of Radcliffe, Maturin, and Lewis. But

Byron takes the already electrifying Gothic villain and eroticizes him with such characters as the Corsair, Lara, and the Giaour. The Brontës place this hero into a narrative of redemptive love. The evil lover is then appropriated by the twentieth-century gothic romance: by Du Maurier, Stewart, and their followers. The erotic historical continues to represent and complicate the malevolent seducer who might be saved by love. A second branch of this history that intertwines in a complex way with the Gothic and its history centers on the seducer or the reformed rake. Mr. B of *Pamela,* the reformed rake, and Lovelace of *Clarissa,* the unmitigated seducer, stand as early models of this type of hero. Byron's Childe Harold seduces but is never saved; he becomes the model for Heathcliff and then Dickens's and Eliot's wreckers of women's lives. Dorian Gray continues in this tradition as does the mesmerizing but ultimately deadly attractions of the vampire. Hull's sheik takes this narrative into the twentieth century as does Rhett Butler and later erotic historicals. And then there is the third branch of this history: the dandy. Byron's Don Juan sets the standard for the cynical effete as do the Silver-Fork heroes. Wilde makes of the dandy something sinister, linking him to the evil seducer. Heyer's regency novels pick up this thread, placing the dandy into a redemptive or reformative narrative. And then, as we have seen, elements of the dandy live on in many erotic historical dangerous lovers.

But finally the dangerous lover's meaning comes from those who desire him: those who themselves long as deeply as he does. One must wonder whether or not the dangerous lover can even be seen except through the lens of women's desire. The true meaning of this figure is located in the one who desires him, who constructs him as a mysterious well of passion through her imaginative yearning for infinity. The heroine is haunted by this fantasy she constructs, and she lets this ideal take over her sexual being as a ghost or vampire might; she constructs and then confronts a terrifying coming together with sublime annihilation, dark transcendence, unspeakable acts. She desires and hence creates the unknown, the impossible, the ineffable. She steps into an outside when she takes his hand, an outside that holds the possibility of freedom, of death, of an infinite mourning or an entering into transcendent meaning.

Appendix

$\mathcal{N}arrative$ $\mathcal{T}imeline$

The Gothic Romance, the Erotic Historical Romance, and the Regency Romance

The intricate nature of a history of the dangerous lover—complicated because of his real pervasiveness in so many texts—makes a brief sketch of his history a necessity. This timeline merely touches, point by point, the notable milestones or hallmarks of what becomes quite a crowd. To begin, four ur-historical texts come, not surprisingly, from Shakespeare. The liebestod of *Romeo and Juliet* (ca.1591) pictures love as a pilgrimage or a sea voyaging. In *Richard III* (1592–1594), Shakespeare shapes a hero/villain who combines cruelty with wit and an insatiable will. With *Hamlet* (1600–1601), impotent melancholy and directionless passion are linked with an erotic magnetism. Iago in *Othello* (1604) emanates the purposeless malignancy of the pure enemy that later is woven into the intricate character of the hero/villain.

In Jacobean tragedy (approximately 1607–1633) many tormented, sympathetic reprobates are to be found. Lucifer in Milton's *Paradise Lost* (1667) falls from grace as later dangerous lovers will. Representing wholesale rebellion, he refuses to bow to any power but his own hellish subjectivity. From Mr. B in Samuel Richardson's *Pamela, or Virtue Rewarded* (1740–1741) we take elements of the eroticized villain who transforms, with mundane magic, into the hero because of the purifying effects of the heroine's virtuousness. Mr. B's influence radiates out into the many seduction narratives of the Victorian period and continues to color the twentieth-century erotic historical romance.

Early in this history, two separate limbs branch out from the tree of late-eighteenth- and early-nineteenth-century dangerous lover texts—the gothic line and the dandy line. Byronism makes its appearance in both of these closely related threads. The Gothic novel of the late eighteenth century masters the enigmatic, passionate, and damned villain who threatens the heroine's virtue and even her life. The most important of these figures are Ann Radcliffe's Montoni in *Mysteries of Udolpho* (1794) and Schedoni in *The Italian* (1797), and Ambrosio in Matthew Lewis's *The Monk* (1796).

Maturin's *Melmoth the Wanderer* (1820) takes up numerous themes that become dear to genres of the contemporary romance—such as silence, secrets, imprisonment, and remorse. The demonic and cursed wanderings of these Gothic villains link them to Satan in *Paradise Lost*. Byron's figures that follow most closely the Gothic hero/villain caught up in darkness, in restless torment are Manfred, Lara, the Giaour, the Corsair, and Childe Harold (1812–1817). Love as redemptive for cursed, Cain-like beings becomes an explicit and essential theme to Byron. Lady Caroline Lamb's *Glenarvon* (1816) then appropriates the Byronic figure as a malignant seducer and vampirelike enemy.

Sir Walter Scott brings a world of nostalgia, myth, and preordained tragedy to his blighted, haunted antiheroes—Ravenswood of *The Bride of Lammermore* (1819), George Staunton of *The Heart of Mid-Lothian* (1818), and Captain Cleveland of *The Pirate* (1822). Sir Reginald Glanville in Edward Bulwer-Lytton's *Pelham* (1828), with the abysmal interiority and finely wrought genius of a Manfred, wastes his life away in remorse for seducing and ruining a young woman. Bulwer-Lytton's *Eugene Aram* (1831) becomes attractive to the heroine because of the way his gloomy guilt keeps him awake studying all night long.

The two most famous Byronic hero/villains of the nineteenth century now appear, cursed with transcendental homelessness: Rochester in *Jane Eyre* (1847) and Heathcliff in *Wuthering Heights* (1847). Rochester steps into history as part of a redemptive love narrative, but for Heathcliff redemption stands always just beyond his reach. Other Victorian-era dangerous lovers come from the Iago tradition of meaningless malevolence. Steerforth in *David Copperfield* (1846), Carker in *Dombey and Son* (1847), and Frank Levison in *East Lynne* (1861) follow in this descent of seductive enemies. Stephen Guest in *Mill on the Floss* (1860) is a less vilified seducer, and Sidney Carton in *A Tale of Two Cities* (1859) is only out for self-ruin, yet his willful blightedness and need for redemption bring him firmly into this history.

The anonymous *Teleny* (1890?) repeats the liebestod theme, and the fascination of a doomed and tragic love. In *The Picture of Dorian Gray* (1890) and *Dracula* (1897), the erotic intoxication of Dorian and the vampire lead to the unholy demise of both the dangerous lover and the other.

In the twentieth century, the Gothic genre of the dangerous lover narrative itself divides into two closely intertwined trajectories—the gothic romance on one hand and erotica on the other. The gothic romance reaches its pinnacle with Du Maurier's Gothic rewrite of *Jane Eye*—*Rebecca* (1938). Gothic romances with plots similar to *Rebecca* became very popular from the mid-1950s to the early 1970s with Mary Stewart, Victoria Holt, and others. During the 1970s, the gothic romance went into decline, yet many Gothic themes were carried into two genres—romantic suspense and the erotic historical. Since 2001 the gothic romance has reappeared as a genre.

Returning to the early twentieth century once again, we need to follow the erotica thread mentioned earlier. While closely related to the gothic romance, primarily through its hero who embodies both hero and villain characteristics, erotic romances are not as haunted, guilt-driven, or as tortured as the gothics. Hull's *The Sheik* (1921) stands as a pivotal text for the later "bodice-ripper" with the heroine's seduction and rape by the exotic hero. Many of D. H. Lawrence's heroes are erotically dark (1920–1930), and his theories on liebestod contribute to this trajectory. Rhett Butler in *Gone with the Wind* (1936) represents a sympathetic dissipated rake who attempts reformation through love. A last gesture of the erotic type—the erotic historical romance—emerged out of the decline of the gothic in the 1970s and was inaugurated officially with the publication of Woodiwiss's *The Flame and the Flower* (1972) and Rogers's *Sweet Savage Love* (1974). Erotic historicals continue to be written and read today; their history and influence are still evolving.

The final dangerous lover genre remaining to be briefly traced in this timeline is the dandy one, which also intertwines with the reformed rake narrative. Taking the latter strain first: the reformed rake can be ultimately traced back to Mr. B in *Pamela*. While Darcy in Austen's *Pride and Prejudice* (1813) isn't really a dandy nor is he a rake, he still becomes part of this generic thread because his mild misanthropy and his snobbish sense of the proprieties are "reformed" through his love for Elizabeth. Byronism appears once again as part of the story of the dandy through the cynical, world-weary narrator of *Don Juan* (1819–1824). In the Silver-Fork novel the dandy again appears in such works as Thomas Henry Lister's *Granby* (1826), Disraeli's *Vivian Grey* (1826), and Bulwer-Lytton's *Pelham* (1828). Here the dandy appears as a kind of rebellious genius needing to be brought back into a society of productive work. *Vanity Fair* (1848) ends the Silver-Fork genre by exploding the dandy ideal as merely an empty superciliousness.

The Victorian seduction narratives mentioned above have a place here as well; the malignant seducer is the kind of rake the contemporary romance will redeem. The contemporary regency romance descends from the Silver-Fork and the reformed rake narrative. Georgette Heyer's regencies from 1921 to 1974 exemplify this genre and its hero whose existential emptiness leads him to excessive dissipation and moral and financial ruin. The heroine arrives to "save" him from his abyss and bring him back to an earthly sense of immanent meaning. Another important influence on the erotic historical romance as the heroes often have the same qualities, regencies are still being produced and consumed today, although they are fast disappearing as a romantic subgenre.

Notes

Introduction

1. Reading popular culture as descriptive or symptomatic of core ontological or existential questionings is nothing new. For instance, Slavoj i ek in particular has popularized Hegelian and Lacanian theories by discussing them through the lens of detective fiction, Hitchcock, and Hollywood.

2. Suzanne Valentina Buffamanti traces just such a trajectory; she writes about the Byronic heroine in Radcliffe, Stoker, Alcott, Hawthorne, and Charlotte Brontë in her dissertation, "The Gothic Feminine: Towards the Byronic Heroine." Additionally, Atara Stein has a chapter on female Byronic heroines in film and television in her *The Byronic Hero in Film, Fiction, and Television.*

3. Pamela Regis, Carol Thurston, and others have systematically defended romances against the many criticisms wielded against them, generally by proving how feminist these narratives can be when the heterogeneity of the genre is considered, as well as the way the readers and writers of romance view their practice. The following project is a different one. In her dissertation, "But Are They Any Good? Women Readers, Formula Fiction, and the Sacralization of the Literary Canon," Beth Rapp Young discusses in detail the historical bias against romance and how this marginalization can be linked to both gender and class (because of romance's largely erroneous association with working-class readers). Young questions the hierarchy created between canonical books that warrant "intensive" reading or "vertical" reading—"paying special, focused attention to extraordinary objects"—and those popular or marginalized texts such as romance that permit "extensive" or "horizontal" reading—"one which relies on knowledge of hundreds of texts, and which does not treat any single book as a self-contained system" (5).

Chapter One

1. Carol Thurston creates a useful taxonomy of romance. Most of the categories used here are closely related to hers. Another who struggles to categorize contemporary romance is Yvonne Annette Jocks, in her master's thesis, "Adventure and Virtue: Alternating Emphasis in the Popular Romance Tradition."

2. Many of the romance publishers have a line of contemporaries, such as Zebra Contemporary Romance, Harlequin/Silhouette's Red Dress Ink, Blaze, and American Romance.

3. Most of the major publishers of romance—such as Harlequin/Silhouette, Avon, Leisure, Warner, Dell, Island, and Fawcett—have an erotic historical line.

4. Carol Thurston, Janice Radway in *Reading the Romance,* and Rosemary Guiley in

Love Lines: The Romance Reader's Guide to Printed Pleasures all give the same account of the influence of *The Flame and the Flower* in reshaping the popular romance formula.

5. For further discussion of the play of such elemental opposing forces in the romance, see Linda Barlow in *Dangerous Men and Adventurous Women*.

6. See Thurston, 38.

7. Barthes points to the equivalence between love and war: "Each time a subject 'falls' in love, he revives a fragment of the archaic time when men were supposed to carry off women . . ." (188). And Paglia: "At some level, all love is combat, a wrestling with ghosts" (14).

8. With *The Sheik* Hull invented a new genre: the "sheik romance." Numerous erotic historicals repeat this story point by point: see Johanna Lindsey's *Captive Bride* for an example of an Arab sheik, really an English lord, who kidnaps and rapes an English virgin. And Beatrice Small's *The Kadin* follows the same plot. Other sheik romances: Lynn Wilding, *The Sheikh* ; Alexandra Sellers, *Sheikh's Woman* (New York: Harlequin); Violet Winspear, *The Sheik's Captive.*

9. A strange revenge fantasy occurs at the end of *The Lustful Turk*, however. The harem is dissolved because one of his love slaves cuts off the Dey's penis.

10. Love as a kind of travel will be further explored in chapter 3.

11. The study of sexual daemonism, or a primitive, violent sexuality, is a part of the eroticism of the demon lover. Camille Paglia chronicles this type of sexuality in *Sexual Personae.*

12. Harlequin's "Intrigue" line, dubbed "romantic suspense," stands as the most gothic of the other romance genres. Furthermore, in addition to their gothic line, Dorchester's "Love Spell" includes romances that contain elements of other genres such as the fairy tale; futuristic themes—heroes who are aliens from other planets; sorcery— a heroine who is a genie, or a hero who is a wizard; the "paranormal"; and time travel.

13. Before Dorchester's gothics, started in 2001, gothic romances in their purity had disappeared from the market since the 1970s. Not surprisingly, given their emphasis on suspense and the desire to disclose a murderous secret, the gothic romance evolved out of the decline of the mystery in the 1950s. As the sales of the mystery story waned in the 1950s, mass-market publishers began looking for a new popular formula. Gerald Gross at Ace Books, remembering the success of Daphne Du Maurier's *Rebecca* (1938) and hoping to attract a large audience of female readers, searched for other titles already published that followed the formula of *Rebecca.* He brought out Phyllis Whitney's *Thunder Heights* in 1960, launching a new "gothic" series. At the same time, Doubleday issued another *Rebecca* formula in 1960, Victoria Holt's *Mistress of Mellyn*, beginning a hugely popular gothic revival. See Radway, *Reading the Romance,* especially page 31; Thurston, *The Romance Revolution,* especially pages 41–44; and Pamela Regis, *A Natural History of the Romance Novel.* For a discussion of Harlequin's move from mysteries, Westerns, and thrillers to romance, see Kay Mussell and Johanna Tunon, eds., *North American Romance Writers.* Mary Stewart must also be mentioned here as an important gothic romance writer. Between 1955 and 1967 she produced ten gothic romances, most of them containing importantly dark and willful heroes who are "tamed" by hardheaded, clear-sighted heroines.

14. Phyllis A. Whitney has been called the "Queen of American Gothic" by the *New York Times.* She has written over sixty mysteries and gothic romances. Another carry-over of the Gothic mode is the gothic which is not a romance. An example is the film *Gaslight* where the lover truly is a villain and nothing but.

15. The obvious historical relatedness of these plots and *Jane Eyre*'s influence on the contemporary gothic romance has been discussed by many; see particularly Thurston, chapters 1–2, and Tania Modleski, especially chapters 1–3.

16. As has been argued about *Jane Eyre,* often the heroine's search to read the hero is a search for her own dark depths, her perhaps angry, sexual, insane, powerful, and free side, expressed by the hero, her double. To some extent, the dangerous lover always acts as a placeholder for desire. An investigation of this would be another historical trajectory entirely, one that waits to be written. An analogy is Gilbert and Gubar's *Madwoman in the Attic,* which charts the ways Jane's anger and sexuality are expressed through Bertha as her double. Also, Laura Kinsdale discusses the hero as double for the heroine in contemporary romance in *Dangerous Men and Adventurous Women.*

17. Alice Eleanor Hibbert has written over two hundred popular romances under six pseudonyms. She is most famously known under three names; she writes "romantic suspense" under Victoria Holt, family sagas under Phillippa Carr, and historical fiction under Jean Plaidy.

18. Barbara Bowman contrasts Holt's rakish hero with an ideal father figure, and the way the heroine must accept the rake in order to become individuated from the father. See *The Female Gothic.*

19. Regencies are still being written today; their major publishers are Zebra, Signet, and Jove. Two important contemporary regency romance writers are Mary Jo Putney and Barbara Cartland.

20. Georgette Heyer (1902–1974) wrote historical romances from 1921–1974. A general consensus among historians of popular romance holds that Georgette Heyer invented the regency romance. Pamela Regis points out that Heyer's "influence is felt in every historical romance written since 1921" (125).

21. This Signet Regency Romance, which has all the hallmarks of the regency formula, is set in eighteenth-century Paris. While this setting may seem odd, it expresses the contemporary use of the word "regency" to represent aristocratic, luxuriant dissipation rather than an actual historical period.

22. The erotic relationship with one's page dates back at least to Byron, who had homosexual relations with his pages. During and after Lady Caroline Lamb's affair with Byron, she would dress up as his page, finally as a frenzied attempt to gain access to him after he refused to see her. She is also reputed to have written most of *Glenarvon* in a page uniform. The page uniform also appears in Victorian pornography as the mark of the "slave" in a sadomasochistic sexual liaison.

23. This mapping of appropriation is similar to the way French writers of the nineteenth century appropriated Byron to create their dandies. Domna Stanton discusses two Byronic models in relation to the French dandy. He is a combination of Harold, Lara, Conrad, and Manfred, creating "the dandy's hidden essence." From *Don Juan* comes "the apparent self" who exhibits "the elegance, seductiveness, and nonchalance" (Stanton, 37).

24. Hannah Arendt calls Heidegger the "last (we hope) romantic" (quoted in Ettinger, 66).

25. "Diese Durchschnittlichkeit in der Vorzeichnung dessen, was gewagt werden kann und darf, wacht über jede sich vordrängende Ausnahme." " . . . die wir die Einebnung aller Seinsmöglichkeiten nennen."

26. "Deise Näherung tendiert jedoch nicht auf ein besorgendes Verfügbarmachen eines Wirklichen, sondern im verstehenden Näherkommen wird die Möglichkeit des Möglichen nur 'grosser'."

27. "Die nachste Nahe des Seins zum Tode als Möglichkeit ist einem Wirklichen so fern als möglich."

28. According to Pamela Regis's description of the structure of the romance, all romances must have two elements: one or more "barriers" and "the point of ritual death"—"the moment . . . when the union of heroine and hero seems completely impossible. It is marked by death or its simulacrum (for example fainting or illness); by the risk of death; or by any number of images or events that suggest death, however metaphorically" (14).

29. Smith has written six romances for St. Martin's, this one in 1999.

30. Garlock has written twenty-six romances for Avon, this one in 1987.

31. Barthes sees the amorous subject in the light of one for whom there are no facts, but rather only signs that need to be interpreted: "From the lover's point of view, the fact becomes consequential because it is immediately transformed into a sign: it is the sign, not the fact, which is consequential (by its aura)" (*Lover's Discourse,* 63).

32. In *Heidegger: On Being and Acting,* Schürrman discusses the way that the pair "near-far" in Heidegger describes Dasein's spatiality of being-in-the-world and how Dasein's everyday interpretation "covers up" its proper being. See especially pages 222–29 and note 96.

33. Anne Stuart writes for Zebra Books and Harlequin. She has been a published writer of romances for over twenty years.

34. Jo Beverly has written at least ten romances for Topaz, this one in 1998. She has won almost all the various awards that *Romance Times* offers.

35. This and the following quote are from Penny Jordan's trilogy, *The Crightons.* One volume contains the three novels; all about an extended family of handsome men. She writes for Harlequin, and this book was published in 2001. According to the text on the inside cover, she has "over 50 million copies of her books in print and translations in nineteen languages."

36. Avital Ronell shows that love itself is a scene of nonunderstanding in her discussion of the "splendor of unintelligibility" in Schlegel's *Lucinde.* See especially *Stupidity,* pages 146–61.

37. Rogers writes for Avon's "Historical Romance" division. She has published fourteen titles with Avon, this one in 1996.

38. Smith has written approximately six romances for St. Martin's, this one in 2001. She is the winner of the "Reviewer's Choice Award for Best First Historical" from *Romantic Times.*

Chapter Two

1. Mario Praz writes a history of the Romantic interest in the morbid and evil. "The very objects which should induce a shudder—the livid face of the severed head, the squirming mass of vipers, the rigidity of death, the sinister light, the repulsive animals, the lizard, the bat—all these give rise to a new sense of beauty, a beauty imperiled and contaminated, a new thrill" (26).

2. See in particular Tania Modleski and David Richter. A good source for a discussion of these types is Clarence Valentine Boyer's *The Villain as Hero in Elizabethan Tragedy.* Kay Mussell argues that *Pamela* is the most important early influence on the contemporary romance.

3. See following chapters for some of the checkered history of the reformed rake genre.

4. In *The Postcard*, Derrida discusses how the proper meaning of language never "arrives," like a dead letter.

5. Richardson's *Clarissa* (1747–48) is a seduction narrative but not a reformed rake one, because Lovelace, the unredeemable rakehell lover, rapes Clarissa, ultimately causing her demise.

6. In *The Female Thermometer*, Terry Castle argues that Radcliffe's lovers are those who mourn for the living, what she calls the "spectralization of the other."

7. As many have argued, the Gothic genre, while not exactly formulaic, is like the mass-market romance because it is made up of such a clear set of conventions that one could make a list of them and find most of them included in every Gothic novel of the time period. For a further discussion of this, see Sedgwick, *The Coherence of Gothic Conventions*, as well as Montague Summers, *The Gothic Quest*.

8. In *Dictations*, Avital Ronell describes writing as always haunted by the master and by self-loss. Elisabeth Bronfen, in *Over Her Dead Body: Death, Femininity, and the Aesthetic*, links storytelling with death, and the reader with a deathlike state. David Punter in *Spectral Readings: Towards a Gothic Geography* argues that "all writing is 'haunted' by the shapes of all that it is not." For a similar argument, see Lucie J. Armitt's "Ghosts and Hauntings in the Victorian Novel."

9. For a more complete discussion of Benjamin's idea of nonlinear history, see Howard Eiland in his foreword to the *Arcades Project*.

10. Praz believes the attraction of the pained, the pale, and the sickly is a device of Romanticism itself: "For the Romantics beauty was enhanced by exactly those qualities which seem to deny it, by those objects which produce horror; the sadder, the more painful it was, the more intensely they relished it" (27).

11. Barthes writes of love as mourning for the other: "The true act of mourning is not to suffer from the loss of the loved object; it is to discern one day, on the skin of the relationship a certain tiny stain, appearing there as the symptom of a certain death" (*Lover's Discourse*, 108).

12. Emily Brontë's poetry contains all these themes as well—love as mourning, the melancholy dangerous lover, the beloved who is imprisoned and then dies.

13. A writer for the nineteenth-century magazine *Godey's Lady's Book* comments that hair is "at once the most delicate and lasting of our materials and survives us like love."

14. Paglia describes this as Heathcliff and Catherine seeking "sadomasochistic annihilation of their separate identities" (448).

15. "Das Noch-nicht ist schon in ihr eigenes Sein einbezogen und das keineswegs als beliebige Bestimmung, sondern als Konstitutivum. Entsprechend ist auch das Dasein, solange es ist, je schon sein Noch-nicht."

16. In *Crack Wars*, Ronell points to the way that addiction creates a temporal inertia when the subject is caught up in only what is immediately available. See especially pages 40–45.

17. "Sobald ein Mensch zum Leben kommt, sogleich ist er alt genug zu sterben."

18. We can see Heideggerian proximity here again: "Thus Dasein proceeds in two directions at once—approaching the source of its being as it draws away from it toward its death" (Fynsk, 51).

19. See Fynsk, who discusses the way the other becomes the source of one's own nullity, especially page 49.

20. Barthes calls this "languor": "Desire for the absent being and desire for the present being: languor superimposes the two desires, putting absence within presence. Whence a state of contradiction: this is the 'gentle fire'" (*Lover's Discourse*, 156).

21. For further discussion of links between *Pride and Prejudice* and contemporary romance, see Modleski.

22. There are hundreds of Pirate erotic historicals; a few are Connie Mason's *Pirate*, Sabrina Jeffries' *The Pirate Lord*, and Jayne Ann Krentz's *The Pirate*. Yvonne Annette Jocks argues that the erotics of piracy date back to the Greek romance.

Chapter Three

1. On the lover's absence, Barthes writes, "The other is in a condition of perpetual departure, of journeying; the other is, by vocation, migrant, fugitive . . ." (*Lover's Discourse*, 13).

2. See Thorslev's book on the Byronic hero and his discussion of how Byron comes out of the tradition of the exiled wanderer.

3. Odysseus in *The Odyssey:*

> I long for home, long for the sight of home.
> If any god has marked me out again
> For shipwreck, my tough heart can undergo it.
> What hardship have I not long since endured
> At sea, in battle! Let the trial come. (5.229–33)

More contemporary to Byron, the wanderer is part of the Romantic tradition of the quest-poem, such as Shelley's Alastor and Keats's Endymion.

4. For instance, in Charles Maturin's *Melmoth the Wanderer,* Mathew Lewis's *The Monk,* James Hogg's *Confessions of a Justified Sinner,* and Mary Shelley's *Frankenstein.*

5. Barthes points out that, since Christianity, the "subject *is the one who suffers*" (*Lover's Discourse*, 189).

6. His story would have been familiar to British readers in Byron's time, if not before: William Johnson Neale's 1840 novel, *The Flying Dutchman,* refers to what appears to be a well-known myth. Frederick Marryat also plays with the myth in his 1839 novel, *The Phantom Ship.*

7. See Caroline Franklin's exploration of the Byronic figure's lovers in *Byron's Heroines.*

8. See particularly Elfenbein's *Byron and the Victorians* for Byronic heroes in the Brontës' juvenilia.

9. In his discussion of Byron's *Cain* and *Heaven and Earth,* William P. Fitzpatrick points out that "the inborn desire for the lost paradise brings about in man a perpetual recurrence of the initial fall" (616).

10. Many before me have discussed the Byronic figure in the Brontës. It is well documented that the Brontës appropriated Byron's poetry and life into the juvenilia and their adult novels and poetry. See especially Gilbert and Gubar's discussion of the Byronic hero in Emily Brontë's poetry, her juvenilia, and in *Wuthering Heights.* They see Heathcliff as a Manfred, and they argue that the union of both Manfred/Astarte and Heathcliff/Catherine create an empowering "androgyne." Stevie Davies discusses incest and the outcast in Byron's mystery plays and *Wuthering Heights.* Elfenbein points out the Byronic characters, primarily females, in Emily's poems.

11. Numerous mass-market romance dark lovers carry the mark of Cain. In the first novel in Harlequin's "[Men Who Are] Dangerous to Love" miniseries, Bonnie Gardner's *Stranger in Her Bed* (1999), the hero, T. J. Swift, has an "angry scar that angled from his right eyebrow and plowed a furrow across his brow and hid in his thick hair" (10). The scar represents his mysterious and guilty past and the deep remorse felt because of his role in the accidental death of his first wife and his son. Having a past that shows in "hard lines of experience" (Smith, 5) perpetuates the erotic hiddenness of pain while making this depth naked, exposed. Until saved by the love of the heroine, he is cursed to feel he has no home in the world, that living itself is his punishment for past errors.

12. From *Ecce Homo:* "I have no word, only a glance, for those who dare to pronounce the word 'Faust' in the presence of Manfred" (254).

13. To view this subject from the position of the lover is to see this sublimity as an *atopos* in the Barthesian sense: "The loved being is recognized by the amorous subject as 'atopos' . . . i.e., unclassifiable, of a ceaselessly unforeseen originality" (*Lover's Discourse,* 34).

14. The time of dangerous love follows the structure of amorous temporality in Proust. Swann is, for the most part, in love with Odette after she has already fallen out of love with him and it is this distance which, at least up to a certain point, increases his love for her. When he hears Vintueil's sonata at Mme De Saint-Euvert's party he has an involuntary memory, suddenly remembering with great pain those days when Odette was in love with him which he characterizes as "the forgotten strains of happiness" (Proust 1: 447). Yet when those days were present Swann was rarely happy in them; there was more often indifference and/or various kinds of pains and jealousies. Through this involuntary memory he is able to finally feel the happiness of being in love and being loved at the same time—the lover and the beloved together. Time is regained and then lost forever: "In place of the abstract expressions 'the time when I was happy,' 'the time when I was loved,' which he had often used until then, and without much suffering, for his intelligence had not embodied in them anything of the past save fictitious extracts which preserved none of the reality, he now recovered everything that had fixed unalterably the peculiar, volatile essence of that lost happiness; he could see it all" (Proust: 1:447).

15. Frances Wilson sees Ladislaw as a "motherless and malcontented Childe Harold who wanders through Europe and the Midlands" (1).

16. This famous quote has been cited by many. Heidegger quotes it in *The Fundamental Concepts of Metaphysics,* and explains that "to be at home everywhere" means to be "within the whole," and this "whole" is the "world." "We are always called upon by something as a whole" (5). Lukács begins his *Theory of the Novel* with this quote. "That is why philosophy, as a form of life or as that which determines the form and supplies the content of literary creation, is always a symptom of the rift between 'inside' and 'outside,' a sign of the essential difference between the self and the world, the incongruence of soul and deed" (29).

17. Bertrand Russell has a chapter on Byron in his *History of Western Philosophy* because he feels that Byronism is important to philosophy in general, especially in the thinking of Nietzsche's *Übermensch.*

18. As a philosopher, the Byronic hero would fall under Klossowski's category of the "philosopher-villain," like Sade. The philosopher-villain sees thinking as a part of his strong passions, as a means to fulfill these passions, whereas the philosopher-decent man understands thinking as of value in and of itself. See *Sade My Neighbor.*

19. We can connect this to Lukács's more sweeping statement: "Defeat is the precondition of subjectivity" (117).

20. In his discussion of Heathcliff as a disruption of the narrative of *Wuthering Heights,* Steve Vine comments that "Heathcliff's narrative function is to open up fixed meanings and identities to otherness . . . invading the seemingly self-identical and turning it inside out" (95).

21. Emily Brontë also would often quit eating, which many have pointed to as a kind of self-destructive protest, a demand for freedom. Steve Vine argues, "Brontë inscribed her desire on her flesh as hunger—and her body became, in the absence of speech, the very text of her deprivation" (20). See also Katherine Frank's *Emily Brontë: A Chainless Soul.*

22. As Kant puts it, the sublime awakens in us the "feeling of a destiny that exceeds completely the domain of the imagination" (quoted in *Sublime,* 140).

23. Paglia traces the theme of incest and sexual, narcissistic doubling throughout Romanticism.

24. Elfenbein points to Byronism's representation of sexuality as a "linkage of eroticism and the confessional mode fulfilled" (18).

25. Susan Stewart's *On Longing: Narratives of the Miniature, the Gigantic, the Souvenir, the Collection* continues this discourse on the interiority of reading spaces and subjects.

26. Roland Barthes is the best articulator of the eroticism of reading; see especially *The Pleasure of the Text.*

27. See especially the Combray section of *In Search of Lost Time,* his essay *On Reading,* and Paul de Man's discussion of reading in Proust in his *Allegories of Reading: Figural Language in Rousseau, Nietzsche, Rilke, and Proust.*

28. See Leslie Marchand's *Byron: A Biography,* 38–39.

29. Byronism strongly influenced Pushkin's *Eugene Onegin.* For representations of Byron in books, films, and theater, see *Byromania,* especially pages 221–29.

Chapter Four

1. Other similarities between these two popular genres should be noted. Both are excessively formulaic, and the Silver-Fork, after an early period of experimentation, was produced by the publisher Henry Colburn in an assembly-line fashion, similar to the contemporary mass-produced romance. Also, both display an obsessive attention to minute details of clothing, food, and other material goods.

2. We can find such reform in Dickens. In many of his developmental narratives, specifically those of Pip and David Copperfield, final earnestness is prefigured by the knowledge and guidance of wiser heroines—Biddy and Agnes, respectively.

3. See Dorian Gray's dandyism later in this chapter.

4. In *Edward Bulwer-Lytton: The Fiction of New Regions,* Allan Conrad Christensen details Bulwer's devastation upon Byron's death, his affair with Byron's ex-mistress Lady Caroline Lamb, and the repetition of this character in his writing. Other dandified literary figures who brought these interests into their fictions were Disraeli, Dickens, and Wilde.

5. The prototypical Byronic hero in *Pelham* is Sir Reginald Glanville. *Eugene Aram, The Haunted and the Haunters,* and *Falkland* also center on Gothic, tormented heroes (see chapter 3 for a discussion of these characters).

6. *Vivian Grey* was described upon its publication as a "sort of Don Juan in prose" (quoted in Wilson, 81).

7. Matthew Whiting Rosa created the classifications of the intellectual and the picturesque dandy.

8. James Eli Adams, in *Dandies and Desert Saints: Styles of Victorian Masculinity*, discusses the dandy as a man of letters in Dickens, Carlyle, and Tennyson.

9. Pushkin's Eugene Onegin also goes the way of melancholy.

10. Trollope treats the Byronic Corsair with levity and satire in *The Eustace Diamonds* (1872). Lizzie Eustace longs for a Corsair and finds one, at least for a while, in Lord George. But, pointing to the Byron of Don Juan rather than the Corsair; he is not an erotic or even romantic figure. Lord George appears to *play* the role of the Corsair, as he would play a comedic part. An example of Lizzie's hardheaded conniving about her "romantic" Corsair: "But these Corsairs are known to be dangerous, and it would not be wise that she should sacrifice any future prospects of importance on behalf of a feeling, which, no doubt, was founded on poetry, but which might too probably have no possible beneficial result. As far as she knew, the Corsair had not even an island of his own in the Aegean Sea . . ." (130).

11. *Pelham* manages to have it all, attracting readers who want to understand and be a part of fashionable life while subtly critiquing this life as well.

12. For discussion of the class element in these seduction narratives, see Anne Clarke's "The Politics of Seduction in English Popular Culture, 1748–1848."

13. The seduction narrative at the heart of *East Lynne* contains a similar condemnation of the dissipated rake as the narratives mentioned in the previous paragraph, yet the class element is different; Levison's most important seduction is of Lady Isabel.

14. Yet Gillian Beer argues the opposite: that the choice of Stephen for Maggie would be one that parallels social forms. The lack of agreement of Stephen's status in society mirrors that of the prototypical dangerous lover who generally has all the power of cultural capital yet is also in some way exiled or outside.

15. *Can You Forgive Her?* and *A Tale of Two Cities* also contain the two-lover narrative, with Carton and Vavasor as the antiheroes. See the discussion of them in chapter 3.

16. See Holland's "Undead Byron," especially pages 155–56.

Works Cited

Abrams, M. H. *Natural Supernaturalism: Tradition and Revolution in Romantic Literature*. New York: Norton, 1971.

Adams, James Eli. *Dandies and Desert Saints: Styles of Victorian Masculinity*. Ithaca, NY: Cornell University Press, 1995.

Armitt, Lucie J. "Ghosts and Hauntings in the Victorian Novel." In *A Companion to the Victorian Novel*, edited by William Baker and Kenneth Womak, 151–61. London: Greenwood Press, 2002.

Austen, Jane. *Persuasion. The Complete Novels of Jane Austen*. New York: Modern Library, n.d.

———. *Pride and Prejudice. The Complete Novels of Jane Austen*. New York: Modern Library, n.d.

———. *Sense and Sensibility. The Complete Novels of Jane Austen*. New York: Modern Library, n.d.

Ballaster, Ros. *Seductive Forms: Women's Amatory Fiction from 1684 to 1740*. New York: Oxford University Press, 1992.

Barlow, Linda, and Jayne Ann Krentz. "Beneath the Surface: The Hidden Codes of Romance." In *Dangerous Men and Adventurous Women*, edited by Jayne Ann Krentz, 15–29. Philadelphia: University of Pennsylvania Press, 1992.

Barthes, Roland. *A Lover's Discourse: Fragments*. Translated by Richard Howard. New York: Farrar, Strauss and Giroux, 1979.

———. *The Pleasure of the Text*. Translated by Richard Miller. New York: Blackwell, 1990.

Becnel, Rexanne. *Dangerous to Love*. New York: St. Martin's, 1997.

Beer, Gillian. *George Eliot*. Bloomington: Indiana University Press, 1986.

Belsey, Catherine. *Desire: Love Stories in Western Culture*. New York: Blackwell, 1994.

Benjamin, Walter. *The Arcades Project*. Translated by Howard Eiland and Kevin McLaughlin. London: Harvard University Press, 2002.

———. *Illuminations*. Edited by Hannah Arendt. New York: Schocken, 1969.

Beverley, Jo. *Lord of Midnight*. New York: Topaz, 1998.

———. *Selected Writings*. Vols. 1–2. Edited by Michael Jennings, Howard Eiland, and Gary Smith. Translated by Rodney Livingstone et al. Cambridge, MA: Harvard University Press, 1999.

Blanchot, Maurice. *The Infinite Conversation*. Translated by Susan Hanson. Minneapolis: University of Minnesota Press, 1993.

———. *The Space of Literature*. Translated by Ann Smock. Lincoln: University of Nebraska Press, 1982.

Bowman, Barbara. "Victoria Holt's Romances: A Structuralist Inquiry." In *The Female Gothic*, edited by Juliann Fleenor, 69–81. London: Eden Press, 1983.

Boyer, Clarence Valentine. *The Villain as Hero in Elizabethan Tragedy*. New York: Russell and Russell, 1964.

Brisman, Leslie. "Byron: Troubled Stream from a Pure Source." *ELH* (*English Literary History*) 42, no. 4 (1975): 623–50.

Bronfen, Elisabeth. *Over Her Dead Body: Death, Femininity, and the Aesthetic.* Manchester: Manchester University Press, 1992.

Brontë, Charlotte. *Jane Eyre.* New York: Penguin Classics, 1989.

Brontë, Emily. *Complete Poems.* New York: Penguin Classics, 1989.

———. *Wuthering Heights.* New York: Penguin Classics, 1989.

Brooks, Peter. *Reading for the Plot: Design and Intention in Narrative.* New York: Knopf, 1984.

Buffamanti, Suzanne Valentina. "The Gothic Feminine: Towards the Byronic Heroine." PhD diss., Purdue University, 2000.

Bulwer-Lytton, Edward. *Eugene Aram.* New York: Kensinger Publishing, n.d.

———. *Pelham or the Adventures of a Gentleman.* New York: Kensinger Publishing, n.d.

Burke, Edmund. *On the Sublime and Beautiful.* Charlottesville, VA: Ibis, 1987.

Byron, George Gordon. *Byron's Poetry.* New York: Norton, 1978.

———. *The Complete Poetical Works.* Boston: Houghton Mifflin, 1905.

———. *Lord Byron's Selected Letters and Journals.* Edited by Leslie Marchand. Cambridge, MA.: Harvard University Press, 1982.

Carlyle, Thomas. *Carlyle's Complete Works.* Vol. 1 of 10. New York: Lovell, n.d.

Castle, Terry. *The Female Thermometer: Eighteenth-Century Culture and the Invention of the Uncanny.* New York: Oxford University Press, 1995.

Christensen, Allan Conrad. *Edward Bulwer-Lytton: The Fiction of New Regions.* Athens: University of Georgia Press, 1976.

Clarke, Anne. "The Politics of Seduction in English Popular Culture, 1748–1848." In *The Progress of Romance: The Politics of Popular Fiction,* edited by Jean Radford, 47–70. London: Routledge, 1986.

Cohn, Jan. *Romance and the Erotics of Property: Mass-Market Fiction for Women.* London: Duke University Press, 1988.

Coleridge, Samuel Taylor. *Poetical Works.* Princeton, NJ: Princeton University Press, 2001.

Coulter, Catherine. *Lord of Hawkfell Island.* New York: Jove, 1993.

Davies, Stevie. *Emily Brontë.* Bloomington: Indiana University Press, 1988.

Deleuze, Gilles, and Félix Guattari. *Kafka: Toward a Minor Literature.* Minneapolis: University of Minnesota Press, 1986.

———. *Proust and Signs.* Translated by Richard Howard. Minneapolis: University of Minnesota Press, 2000.

Derrida, Jacques. *The Postcard: From Socrates to Freud and Beyond.* Translated by Alan Bass. Chicago: University of Chicago Press, 1987.

Derrida, Jacques, and Maurizio Ferraris. *A Taste for the Secret.* Translated by Giacomo Donis. Maldon, MA: Blackwell, 2001.

Dickens, Charles. *David Copperfield.* New York: Dodd, Mead, 1943.

———. *Dombey and Son.* New York: Penguin Classics, 1985.

———. *Tale of Two Cities.* Chicago: Scott, Foresman, 1919.

Disraeli, Benjamin. *Vivian Grey.* London: R. Brimley Johnson, 1904.

Doyle, Elizabeth. *My Lady Pirate.* New York: Kensington, 2001.

Du Maurier, Daphne. *Rebecca.* New York: Modern Library, 1938.

Eisler, Benita. *Byron: Child of Passion, Fool of Fame.* New York: Knopf, 1999.

Elfenbein, Andrew. *Byron and the Victorians.* Cambridge: Cambridge University Press, 1996.

———. "Silver-Fork Byron and Regency England." In *Byromania: Portraits of the Artist in Nineteenth- and Twentieth-Century Culture,* edited by Frances Wilson, 77–92. New York: St. Martin's, 1999.

Eliot, George. *Middlemarch.* New York: Modern Library, 2001.

———. *Mill on the Floss.* New York: Norton, 1994.

Eliot, T. S. *Selected Essays.* New York: Harcourt, Brace, 1932.

Ettinger, Elzbieta. *Arendt and Heidegger.* New Haven, CT: Yale University Press, 1995.

Fitzpatrick, William P. "Byron's Mysteries: The Paradoxical Drive toward Eden." *Studies in English Literature, 1500–1900* 15, no. 4 (1975): 615–25.

Franklin, Caroline. *Byron's Heroines.* New York: Oxford, 1992.

Freud, Sigmund. "The Uncanny" and "Mourning and Melancholia." *Collected Papers.* Vol. 4. Translated by Joan Riviere. New York: Basic Books, 1959.

Fynsk, Christopher. *Heidegger: Thought and Historicity.* Ithaca, NY: Cornell University Press, 1993.

Gardner, Bonnie. *Stranger in Her Bed.* New York: Silhouette, 1997.

Garlock, Dorothy. *Wind of Promise.* New York: Warner, 1987.

Gasche, Rodolphe, and Mark Taylor, eds. *Of the Sublime: Presence in Question.* Albany: State University of New York Press, 1993.

Gilbert, Sandra, and Susan Gubar. *The Madwoman in the Attic: The Woman Writer and the Nineteenth-Century Literary Imagination.* New Haven, CT: Yale University Press, 1979.

Godwin, William. *The Adventures of Caleb Williams or Things as They Are.* New York: Holt, Rinehart and Winston, 1965.

Guiley, Rosemary. *Love Lines: The Romance Reader's Guide to Printed Pleasures.* New York: Facts on File, 1983.

"Hair Ornaments." *Godey's Lady's Book* 2, no.10 (1860): 187.

Harlequin Website. Harlequin Enterprises Limited 2000–2003. October 30, 2003. www.eharlequin.com.

Hayden, John, ed. *Romantic Bards and British Reviewers: A Selected Edition of the Contemporary Reviews of the Works of Wordsworth, Coleridge, Byron, Keats, and Shelley.* London: Routledge, 1971.

Heidegger, Martin. *Being and Time.* Translated by Joan Stambaugh. Albany: State University of New York Press, 1996.

———. *The Fundamental Concepts of Metaphysics.* Translated by William McNeill and Nicholas Walker. Bloomington: Indiana University Press, 1995.

Heine, Heinrich. *From the Memoirs of Herr von Schnabelewopski.* Translated by Charles Godfrey Leland. Vol. 1 of *The Works of Heinrich Heine.* 11 vols. London: W. Heinemann, 1891–1905.

Heyer, Georgette. *These Old Shades.* New York: Signet, 1988.

———. *Venetia.* London: Pan, 1958.

Hogg, James. *The Private Memoirs and Confessions of a Justified Sinner.* New York: Grove, 1959.

Hölderlin, Friedrich. *Essays and Letters on Theory.* Translated by Thomas Pfau. New York: State University of New York Press, 1988.

Holland, Tom. "Undead Byron." In *Byromania,* edited by Frances Wilson, 154–65. New York: St. Martin's, 1999.

Holt, Victoria. *Mistress of Mellyn.* Greenwich, CT: Fawcett Crest, 1960.

Homer. *The Odyssey.* Translated by Robert Fitzgerald. New York: Everyman, 1992.

Hull, Edith. *The Sheik.* Philadelphia: Pine Street Books, 2001.

Humpherys, Anne. "Dombey and Son: Carker the Manager." *Nineteenth-Century Fiction* 34, no. 4 (1980): 397–413.

Jackson, Lisa. *Devil's Gambit.* New York: Silhouette, 1985.

Jocks, Yvonne Annette. "Adventure and Virtue: Alternating Emphasis in the Popular Romance Tradition." Master's thesis, University of Texas at Arlington, 1988.

Jordan, Penny. *The Crightons.* New York: Harlequin, 2001.

Kamuf, Peggy. *Book of Addresses.* Stanford, CA: Stanford University Press, 2005.

Kant, Immanuel. *The Critique of Judgment.* Translated by J. H. Bernard. Amherst, NY: Prometheus Books, 2000.

Keats, John. *Complete Poetical Works.* Boston: Houghton Mifflin, 1966.

King, Margaret, and Elliot Engel. "The Emerging Carlylean Hero in Bulwer's Novels of the 1830s." *Nineteenth Century Fiction* 36, no. 3 (1981): 277–95.

Kinsdale, Laura. "The Androgynous Reader: Point of View in the Romance." In *Dangerous Men and Adventurous Women,* edited by Jayne Ann Krentz, 31–44. Philadelphia: University of Pennsylvania Press, 1992.

Klossowski, Pierre. *Sade My Neighbor.* Translated by Alphonso Lingis. London: Quartet, 1992.

Lacoue-Labarthe, Philippe. *The Literary Absolute.* Albany: State University of New York Press, 1988.

Lamb, Lady Caroline. *Glenarvon.* London: Everyman, 1995.

Lawrence, D. H. *Lady Chatterley's Lover.* New York: Modern Library, 1993.

———. "Love." In *Sex, Literature, and Censorship,* edited by Harry T. Moore, 33–39. New York: Twayne, 1953.

———. *Women in Love.* New York: Modern Library, 1950.

Lewis, Matthew. *The Monk.* New York: Grove, 1959.

Lister, Thomas Henry. *Granby.* New York: Harper, 1826.

Lukács, Georg. *The Theory of the Novel.* Translated by Anna Bostock. Cambridge, MA: MIT Press, 1994.

The Lustful Turk: Scenes in the Harem of an Eastern Potentate. London: Wordsworth, 1995.

Marchand, Leslie. *Byron: A Biography.* New York: Knopf, 1957.

Marcus, Steven. *The Other Victorians.* New York: Basic Books, 1966.

Marryat, Frederick. *The Phantom Ship.* London: Routledge, 1893.

Maturin, Charles. *Melmoth the Wanderer.* Lincoln: University of Nebraska Press, 1961.

McBride, Julie. *Wed to a Stranger?* New York: Harlequin, 1997.

McGann, Jerome. *Byron and Romanticism.* New York: Cambridge University Press, 2002.

Mcleod, Jock. "Misreading Writing: Rousseau, Byron, and Childe Harold III." *Comparative Literature* 43, no. 3 (1991): 260–79.

Milton, John. *Paradise Lost.* New York: Penguin, 2000.

Mitchell, Margaret. *Gone with the Wind.* New York: Macmillan, 1936.

Mitchell, Sally. *The Fallen Angel: Chastity, Class and Women's Reading.* Bowling Green, OH: Bowling Green Popular Press, 1981.

Modleski, Tanya. *Loving with a Vengeance.* New York: Routledge, 1994.

Moers, Ellen. *The Dandy: Brummell to Beerbohm.* New York: Viking Press, 1960.

Mussell, Kay, and Johanna Tunon, eds. *North American Romance Writers.* London: Scarecrow, 1999.

Nancy, Jean-Luc. *The Inoperative Community.* Minneapolis: University of Minnesota Press, 1991.

———. *Of the Sublime: Presence in Question.* Albany: State University of New York Press, 1993.

Neale, Johnson. *The Flying Dutchman.* London: Thomas Tegg, 1840.

Nietzsche, Friedrich. *Collected Writings.* Translated by Walter Kaufmann. New York: Modern Library, 2000.

Novalis. *Philosophical Writings.* Translated and edited by Margaret Stoljar. New York: State University of New York Press, 1997.

Paglia, Camille. *Sexual Personae.* New York: Vintage, 1991.

Polidori, John. *Vampyre. Three Gothic Novels.* Edited by E. F. Bleiler. New York: Dover, 1966.

Praz, Mario. *The Romantic Agony.* Translated by Angus Davidson. New York: Meridian, 1956.

Proust, Marcel. *In Search of Lost Time.* 6 vols. Translated by C. K. Scott Moncrieff and Terence Kilmartin. New York: Modern Library, 1993.

Punter, David. *Spectral Readings: Towards a Gothic Geography.* London: Macmillan, 1999.

Radcliffe, Anne. *The Italian.* London: Folio Society, 1987.

———. *The Mysteries of Udolpho.* London: Dent, 1965.

Radford, Jean, ed. *The Progress of Romance: Politics of Popular Fiction.* New York: Routledge, 1986.

Radway, Janice. *Reading the Romance.* Chapel Hill: University of North Carolina Press, 1991.

Regis, Pamela. *A Natural History of the Romance.* Philadelphia: University of Pennsylvania Press, 2003.

Richardson, Samuel. *Clarissa.* New York: Penguin, 1985.

———. *Pamela.* New York: Houghton Mifflin, 1971.

Richter, David. *The Progress of Romance: Literary Historiography and the Gothic Novel.* Columbus: Ohio State University Press, 1996.

Rickels, Laurence. *Vampire Lectures.* Minneapolis: University of Minnesota Press, 1999.

Roberts, Neil. *George Eliot: Her Beliefs and Her Art.* Pittsburgh, PA: University of Pittsburgh Press, 1975.

Rogers, Evelyn. *Devil in the Dark.* New York: Dorchester, 2001.

———. *The Loner.* New York: Dorchester, 2001.

Rogers, Rosemary. *A Dangerous Man.* New York: Avon, 1996.

———. *Sweet Savage Love.* New York: Mira, 1974.

Ronell, Avital. *Crack Wars: Literature Addiction Mania.* Lincoln: University of Nebraska Press, 1992.

———. *Dictations: On Haunted Writing.* Lincoln: University of Nebraska Press, 1986.

———. *Stupidity.* Chicago: University of Illinois Press, 2002.

Rosa, Matthew Whiting. *The Silver-Fork School: Novels of Fashion Preceding* Vanity Fair. New York: Columbia University Press, 1936.

Russell, Bertrand. *A History of Western Philosophy.* New York: Simon and Schuster, 1945.

Sales, Roger. "The Loathsome Lord and the Disdainful Dame: Byron, Cartland and the Regency Romance." In *Byromania,* edited by Frances Wilson, 166–83.

Schürrman, Reiner. *Heidegger: On Being and Acting: From Principles to Anarchy.* Translated by Christine-Marie Gros. Bloomington: Indiana University Press, 1987.

Scott, Sir Walter. *The Bride of Lammermore*. Philadelphia: Gebbie, 1896.

———. *The Heart of Mid-Lothian*. New York: Penguin, 1994.

———. *The Pirate*. New York: Collier, n.d.

Sedgwick, Eve. *The Coherence of Gothic Conventions*. New York: Methuen, 1986.

———. *Tendencies*. Durham: Duke University Press, 1993.

Shakespeare, William. *Romeo and Juliet*. New York: Arden, 1995.

Smith, Barbara Dawson. *Seduced by a Scoundrel*. New York: St. Martin's, 1999.

Smith, Hayword. *Border Lord*. New York: St. Martin's, 2001.

Stanton, Domna. *The Aristocrat as Art: A Study of the Honnête Homme and the Dandy in Seventeenth- and Nineteenth-Century French Literature*. New York: Columbia University Press, 1980.

Stein, Atara. *The Byronic Hero in Film, Fiction, and Television*. Carbondale: Southern Illinois University Press, 2004.

Stevens, Amanda. *Stranger in Paradise*. New York: Harlequin, 1995.

Stoker, Bram. *Dracula*. New York: Modern Library, n.d.

Stuart, Anne. *Lord of Danger*. New York: Zebra Books, 1997.

Teleny. London: Wordsworth, 1995.

Thackeray, William Makepeace. *Vanity Fair*. New York: Nelson Doubleday, n.d.

Therrien, Kathleen Mary. "Trembling at Her Own Response: Resistance and Reconciliation in Mass-Market Romance Novels." PhD diss., University of Delaware, 1997.

Thorslev, Peter. *The Byronic Hero*. Minneapolis: University of Minnesota Press, 1962.

Thurston, Carol. *The Romance Revolution: Erotic Novels for Women and the Quest for a New Sexual Identity*. Chicago: University of Chicago Press, 1987.

Trollope, Anthony. *Can You Forgive Her?* Hertfordshire, UK: Wordsworth, 1996.

———. *The Eustace Diamonds*. London: Everyman, 1992.

Vine, Steven. *Emily Brontë*. New York: Twayne, 1998.

Wagner, Richard. "The Flying Dutchman." *Grand English Opera*. Dir. C. D. Hess. Translated by Caryl Florio. 1874.

Weiskel, Thomas. *The Romantic Sublime*. Baltimore: Johns Hopkins University Press, 1976.

Welsh, Alexander. *The Hero of the Waverly Novels*. New York: Atheneum, 1968.

Whitney, Phyllis. *Thunder Heights*. New York: Ace Star, 1960.

Wilde, Oscar. *Picture of Dorian Grey*. New York: Books, Inc, 1944.

Wilson, Frances, ed. *Byromania: Portraits of the Artist in Nineteenth- and Twentieth-Century Culture*. New York: St. Martin's, 1999.

Woodiwiss, Kathleen. *The Flame and the Flower*. New York: Avon, 1972.

Wood, Ellen. *East Lynne*. Edited by Andrew Maunder. Peterborough, ON: Broadview, 2000.

Young, Beth Rapp. "But Are They Any Good? Women Readers, Formula Fiction, and the Sacralization of the Literary Canon." PhD diss., University of Southern California, 1995.

Index